HIGH-NOON PLANET

In the detective stories it's always getting dark when the beautiful client shows up. But on the planet Tankur it never gets dark. It's always high noon and hotter than Hell.

"I hear that you rough up people for money," she said, in broad daylight.

Quite frankly, I was shocked. I said: "Depends on how badly you want them roughed up. I also give quantity discounts."

This was at the beginning of the buried-city caper, and I was several days away from discovering how distinctly unfunny that last remark could turn out to be. . . .

Praise for John E. Stith's Previous Novels:

"This futuristic thriller is taut and gripping, the characters are believable, and the computer's pretty human, too!"

—*British Science Fiction Society Newsletter*

"John Stith [has] succeeded where so many others have failed . . . [DEATH TOLL is] respectable both as science fiction and as mystery."

—*The Drood Review of Mystery*

"Entertaining!"
—*Voice of Youth Advocates*

DEEP QUARRY

JOHN E. STITH

ACE BOOKS, NEW YORK

This book is an Ace
original edition, and has
never been previously published.

DEEP QUARRY

An Ace Book/published by arrangement with
the author

PRINTING HISTORY
Ace edition/February 1989

ISBN: 0-441-14276-1

Ace Books are published by The Berkley Publishing Group,
200 Madison Avenue, New York, New York 10016.
The name ''Ace'' and the ''A'' logo
are trademarks belonging to Charter Communications, Inc.

PRINTED IN THE UNITED STATES OF AMERICA

10 9 8 7 6 5 4 3 2 1

For two pivotal people who turned the clock ahead:
Elinor Mavor and Susan Allison

1

Just the Facts, Ma'am

I.
Who Shall I Say Is Calling?

I was so hot and sweaty that the warble from the desk comlink was almost a welcome interruption. Close, but not quite. The tone repeated as I considered my credit balance. Even after coming to the standard conclusion that answering the call was the prudent thing to do, I hesitated. For my taste, far too much bad news takes that path of least resistance.

Finally, I tapped the ANSWER pad, cutting off the tone. We all have to do things we don't like.

A young man's pale face came up in my screen. He had lots of freckles. If sunlight brings out your freckles, Tankur just isn't the place to be. I also noticed that the heat exchanger at his place must have been working better than mine. His skin didn't even look shiny. I was envious.

"Mr. Takent?" he said. His white, short-sleeved shirt bore a flowery "L" on the pocket.

I nodded. This was good. I could answer his first question without even doing any research.

"Kate—" he started. "Oh, just a minute. I've got another call. You mind if I put you on hold?"

My screen went flat and blank before I could even open my mouth to say, "No problem. You mind if I shoot you?"

I hate being put on hold and I really don't like the comlink all that much. One call is worth a thousand advertising handouts. I was sometimes surprised that I had gravitated toward a profession that required so much calling. I sat there staring at the gray rectangle, speculating about whether being put on hold this way might qualify as a trigger for justifiable homicide.

I wiped my forehead slowly and wondered why the people coming to fix the heat exchanger weren't here yet. Life is so full of questions. *That* must be the reason I do what I do; almost everybody is willing to pay for answers.

I leaned back in my chair. My shirt felt like a sheet of rumpled adhesive between the chair and my body. I tried to ignore the feeling as I reviewed a mental image of what had been on the screen. This guy must have been calling from a school. On the low partition wall behind him hung a few framed photos of what seemed to be a campus and a group picture with an advanced-degree seal on it.

A portion of a red emblem had shown near the bottom of one side of the screen. I'd bet it was the upper left corner of the University of Alteson symbol, a stylized blazing red sun. They had a branch here on Tankur, and the call was local; the man's comlink number showed on the status line on top of the screen. I could have had the computer look up the rest of the entry, but it was too hot to bother.

I hoped I was wrong about it being a school. Schools are notorious for paying poorly.

Several minutes later the screen finally lit up again, showing the same smiling man still sitting in his comfortable, cooled room. I leaned forward, my shirt stubbornly coming loose from the chair and making a sound like a zipper.

"Sorry about that," my caller said. "What I was saying was—"

"Oh, excuse me a minute," I interrupted. "There's another call on my line." Before he could say anything, I tapped the HOLD pad.

I sat there a few minutes, feeling better but almost guilty. It was a calculated risk. Sure, maybe I'd alienate a potential client. Sure, I was giving in to a rather pointless urge. But I felt a little happier by the time I tapped the HOLD pad again. Sometimes you just have to go with your feelings.

The man's image snapped back onto my screen. He had

been busy typing something and he pointedly finished the last few seconds of it.

"Sorry," I said with my most winning smile. "Now what were you saying?"

He frowned slightly, just enough to make me think he suspected what I had done. So sue me.

"Kate Dunlet wants to talk to you," he said curtly, as though I should know who she was. "I'll put her on now."

Great. So this guy was just a secretary. And the whole time we had been on hold, Kate whoever had been relaxing in her own office, which I was sure was also properly cooled.

My screen went gray again, this time for maybe ten seconds. When the color came back, a face much more pleasant than the first one was in the screen. She was human, too. Her brown hair was hardly longer than my own and it looked good on her. It didn't quite cover her ears. Her tan didn't fit with the office environment, though. She must work outside a lot.

She was probably about my age. Her light blouse seemed more suitable for outdoors than a cooled office. She looked businesslike, efficient, even before she said a word. Maybe it was her eyes. I wondered vaguely if she were going to call someone else to the phone once *she* verified that it was me.

"Mr. Takent?" she said. "The private investigator?"

"That's me," I said. "What can I—oh say, can you hang on for just a minute? I've got another call."

This time I came even closer to feeling guilty. Maybe she hated the comlink as much as I did. I readjusted the fan on my desk. I would have opened the windows, but it was even hotter outside. It always was on this dust-ball of a planet.

Eternally the optimist, I walked to the door, up a couple of steps, and peered out to see if the heat-exchanger people were in sight yet. They weren't.

The narrow, dusty street outside was sized and angled so the sun's rays never reached the ground, but the air was still warmer than in my two-room office. I was lucky enough to be on the bottom floor, half buried in the sand, so the ground could suck away the heat about as fast as the hot air could force it in. I didn't envy my upstairs neighbor his utility charges. But then he didn't have to shovel the dirt out of his doorway twice a week. Or more often if I had clients to impress.

Back at my desk, I waited a shorter time than before and then reconnected the call. I hoped the woman didn't know how remote the odds were that I would get two calls simultaneously.

"Sorry about that," I said when her face was back on my screen. It was a nice face. "Busy, busy, busy."

Her cool gray eyes stared at me for just an instant before she said, "Perhaps too busy for another case?"

I rarely get that busy. But you have to instill in your clients a sense of your value. "It depends on the nature of the case, Ms—"

"Kate Dunlet. I'm with the University of Alteson here in Dallad. We're doing the dig out west of town."

I couldn't remember if being *with* an employer ranked higher than being *from* or *of*, but it must be higher than *employed by* or *work for*. I said, "Go on." It certainly had to be higher than *work at*.

"I'd rather not talk about it on the comlink. How about if we meet?"

"Couldn't you at least tell me a little about the nature of the problem you want help with? So I can decide if I can work it in or not?" I could work it in. But I was curious.

She looked at me long enough to make me wonder if she knew my current workload, but at last she said, "Someone's been threatening me. I want you to find out who it is and rough him up. A friend of mine told me you do that sort of thing."

"You wouldn't be using 'rough up' in the sense of physically abusing him, would you?"

"Yes," she said evenly.

"I thought you probably were."

II.

Don't Try Anything Funny.
This Could Be Serious.

I had to meet Kate Dunlet. Even before she told me what she wanted, my curiosity had been aroused. Now I was even more curious. And maybe a little aroused. I certainly hoped that when we met I could find out why she was lying to me. No one who knew me would even think that I roughed people up unless I was defending myself.

I might have tried to gauge how much I could charge by how willing she was to come to my office, but it was just too hot. I agreed to meet her at a bar between my office and the university. I planned to pick up my skimmer and travel most of the way in comfort.

Just as I was leaving my office, the comlink sounded again. It was the heat-exchanger people calling to say they couldn't make it over today after all. Since it was almost quitting time, I wasn't too surprised.

I strapped on my wristcomp, once again bothered by the need for communications. But if anyone were in a hurry to call me, being available was worth money. At the door, I grabbed a silvery, wide-brimmed hat.

The heat hit hard outside. If I had been starting out from a comfortable temperature, it probably wouldn't have bothered me for fifteen minutes. As it was, I immediately started sweating more heavily. I drew a sharp breath. Luckily, it wasn't hot enough to incinerate my nostril hair.

No one else was out as I walked down the narrow, shadowed street. Dust swirled past my feet and eddies formed near the doorways I passed. Up high I could see the sun-line exactly where it always was. It was hard to tell, since the brilliance above made the shadow below seem almost gloomy, but above the line the original texture of the wall had flattened and faded with continuous exposure to the sun.

There was no help for it, so at the corner I turned left onto a wide street much different from my own. Instantly the sun's direct rays made me hotter.

Few humans lived on this street. The buildings sloped away from the street bottom, making room for terraces at three levels, so people who had much higher temperature tolerances than humans could bask in the sunlight.

And bask they did, at any time of day. I still wasn't perfectly used to it, but the sun gives no clues to the time. Above this hot and dusty city of Dallad, the sun stays fixed in the cloudless sky. Millennia ago, Tankur had slowed down enough that its revolution period matched the orbital period. Sometimes the city seems to be just as slow.

On this street, at least there was some activity besides the rippling of heat waves. People lay sunning on their terraces and kids played quiet games on the ground. Most of the folks out were Derjons. With their love of heat, a lot of them would prefer to be on an even hotter world, but then they'd lose out on commerce with other races. Dallad was primarily a resort town because of the climate, but there was also some heavy-metal mining nearby. Between the sunlight and the dust, I sneezed. It was probably the loudest sound in the last half-hour.

I said "hello" to a few red-faced, spindly Derjon kids I recognized. One of them waved at me with fingers so thin that his hand looked like a skeleton's. I made it to the next intersection before anything happened.

"Hold it right there, mister," said a voice from the shadow just to my right. "Don't try anything funny."

"I don't feel very funny right now anyway," I said, turning toward the voice.

"Freeze," said the voice, insisting.

"Don't I wish," I said. "I'm too hot for this today, Berto."

"What's the matter, man?" Berto asked. He moved out of the shadow and put his pointed finger back at his side. Berto was a Venton. They are a pale, humanoid race, generally shorter than humans. Berto was only two-thirds of my height because he was still a kid. By the time he became an adult, the top of his head might reach my chin. His canines glinted white in the sunshine as he smiled and squinted at me. The sun was bright for his eyes, too.

I explained about the heat-exchanger in my office. "Maybe I'll have more energy tomorrow. You better watch out, though. You try that when I'm worried, and I might needle you."

"You don't even have your gun today, man," Berto said, grinning. "I looked."

Instinctively, I patted my hip. "Damn, you're right. I knew I was forgetting something again."

"You want me to run back and get it for you? I know how to get in."

I really didn't want Berto handling my needler, and the idea of his running in this heat, even if it didn't bother him, made me feel even hotter. "No. I won't need it for this case." If I'm a private eye long enough, maybe I'll eventually be right more often.

"You sure?" Berto didn't conceal his disappointment very well.

"Sorry." As long as I had stopped, I moved into the shade. "But there is something you can do. You can tell me if you've heard anything funny going on over at the university."

This is the time when in a detective melodrama the kid says, "Not much. But they say that Kate Dunlet woman is one to watch out for. Her last five husbands are all dead."

Berto said, "What university, man?"

"You're as useless as a sundial," I said, and Berto grinned.

"I know the university, man. But I haven't heard any good jokes about it. They're just digging for things out in the dessert."

"*Desert*, Berto, *desert*. Dessert is what you eat after dinner."

"Right. Right." Our language came from a merging of human and Venton vocabularies. Berto still had trouble with the words from our side that didn't fit his version of common sense.

"Look, I've got to run," I said. "Or at least keep walking. I'll continue the language lesson another time, OK?"

"OK. See you later, bug eye." Berto waved as he started to run down the street. His pale face seemed almost pure white in the sunlight.

Two blocks away, I got my skimmer out of the parking lot. The seat stung my back as I got in. A covered lot would have made it a good deal more comfortable, but on Tankur it was almost criminal not to take advantage of solar power. If the heat of the skimmer were any indication, the power pack had enough charge to push me to escape velocity.

I drained half the energy by turning the cooler on strong enough to freeze tears, and pulled out silently onto the mirage-laden street. At least I had just enough intuition to *wonder* if this might turn out to be more complex than it seemed to be.

I'd had cases that ran in circles, cases that led straight into dead ends, but never a case that took such a right-angle turn.

III.

And If You Believe That—

Of the hundreds of bars in Dallad, the Dark Tower Bar was one of the few that catered to humans. The atmosphere inside was easily fifteen degrees below body temperature. And it was properly dim. I wouldn't have suggested the place if I hadn't been in dire need of cooling off, but it was an OK bar.

I looked around for Kate Dunlet and didn't see her, but there was no point wasting time so I found a table and ordered a drink. The Derjon waiter who brought it was fairly old; the two knobs on his forehead had darkened with age and his red face had a weathered look. His heavy jacket was well worn. He clicked his appreciation for the tip and I leaned back in a comfortable chair to enjoy. My throat was so hot, the drink hissed as it went down.

Maybe if the heat-exchanger people didn't fix my unit soon, I could just buy a large refrigerator and spend part of the day in it. If I were lucky, I wouldn't even hear the comlink.

I was relaxing, feeling better than I had all day when my wristcomp beeped. "Yes," I said reluctantly.

"Mr. Takent? This is Kate Dunlet. I'm in a booth on the fourth floor. All the way at the end."

"That's nice. I'm at a table. Just to the left of the entrance."

"What I mean is, I'd like you to join me."

"I had a premonition that you were going to say that. I'll be up." I switched off, drained my glass, and got another before climbing the stairs.

Kate Dunlet was where she had said, alone. I nodded at her and sat down. "Much better than downstairs," I said, looking through the tinted glass and out across the city. In the distance, a lake that wasn't there shimmered in the heat.

"Tell me about this guy you want me to physically abuse," I said, not waiting for her reply. "And how much do you expect to pay?"

"I thought the seller usually determined the fee," she said calmly. She wore a high-necked, short-sleeved tan blouse with white piping, tan slacks, and shoes meant for walking rather than show. Her elbows were on the table as she held a drink to her mouth. Her biceps were large enough to show she wasn't lazy but wasn't a muscle-builder either.

I'd play along with her little game for now. "I suppose so. It depends on how many people you want me to rough up. I sometimes give quantity discounts. And if this person turns out to be someone I don't like, it gets even cheaper." I gave her my best sleazy-businessman's smile but she didn't reciprocate. Maybe I was losing my sex appeal. "How about if you tell me the situation?"

She gave me an obviously appraising glance with her clear gray eyes and then started talking. Her voice was smooth and soft. "I'm one of the archaeologists working on the digs out west of town. Maybe you read about the site that was discovered there a few years ago. We're uncovering a village that has been buried under the sand for probably ten thousand years. There's a lot of manual labor involved. We hire almost anyone who's willing to work. The Wompers are maybe the best workers because they're strongest, but we also employ humans, Venton, and Derjons."

"This guy you want me to rough up. He's hired help?"

"He was. I fired him last week. Since then, he's been calling me at all hours, making threats. He's a Womper, so I take him seriously."

"Boy," I said, rubbing my chin. "Wompers are real tough. I might have to charge you extra."

"What do you suggest?"

"Well, I suppose it doesn't have to be all money," I said, leering at her just a little. I didn't like being lied to. Maybe that kind of treatment would stop her.

She swallowed noticeably. "Well, maybe we could work something out."

I drained the last of my drink and set the glass down heavily on the table. "I hate myself sometimes," I said. "I was wondering which one of us was going to quit lying first, and I have to admit I hoped it would be you."

"What are you saying?" Faint horizontal creases formed on her forehead.

"Oh, come on, Ms. Dunlet. You're probably an exceptionally good archaeologist, but you don't do *everything* well. It's nothing to be ashamed of, but you don't lie worth a damn."

"I'm not sure I understand." There was more color in her cheeks now, beneath the tan.

"I'm not sure I do, either. You want me for a job, but you don't want me to rough up anyone, which I wouldn't do anyway. You should have made some reference checks. If you had, you would have learned that I'm painfully honest, and competent. On the comlink you implied that you didn't know the man's identity. Now you do. If you really wanted me to beat someone up, you probably wouldn't have had your secretary place the call. You might not have even given me your right name, which I verified in the university database. Anyone who's at all cautious wouldn't even bring up the subject until she had sized up the potential employee. And you strike me as cautious. Besides all that, I've never known a Womper who could suppress an undeserved guilt complex long enough even to swear at a person."

"Why did you agree to come here then?" she asked, blinking at me.

"For one thing, it must be fifteen degrees cooler here than my office is today. For another I was thirsty."

"That's it?"

"Maybe ten percent of it. I was curious. And I liked the way you looked on the screen. Is that too sexist for you?"

For the first time, she smiled. It was just a slight turning up of the corners of her lips, and a small dimple began to show. I had the feeling that for her it was a fairly unreserved smile. "No," she said. "I like candor."

It took me a moment to stop laughing. I was wiping a tear from my eye, trying to explain, when she added, "I know what you're going to say. This wasn't the most candid way to get you here."

"Before you say anything more, just tell me the job is honest."

She leaned toward me and put her hand flat on the table. "It's honest. It may not be easy, but it's honest."

I watched her closely, and she convinced me. I reached forward to order another drink with the table pad.

"OK," I said. "How much of what you said was true besides your name?"

"We are doing the dig. And we do employ quite a few workers." She pushed her own drink to one side. "I need help. And I need someone honest. That's why the charade—to see if you would do something illegal for money. The people I asked about you said good things, but I guess I was having a hard time convincing myself that if you were honest you wouldn't be working on a better-paying world or for a large outfit.''

"The job," I said.

"First, I've got a question. Why do they call you 'bug eye'? You look pretty good, with the possible exception of your nose. And it gives you character.''

"I'm not sure whether it's a flattering name or not, but it comes from the fact that besides being a private eye, I seem to do my best when the case involves non-humans.''

"I'm sorry?" she said, shaking her head and looking puzzled.

"There are still a few bigots around who use the term 'bug-eyed monster' to mean people who don't happen to be human.''

She smiled ruefully as she made the connection. "To tell you the truth, I'm not sure if this problem involves non-humans or not. Do you take *only* cases involving other races?''

"No reverse bigotry here, either. Tell me what you need.''

"OK," she said, settling back in her chair, apparently deciding where to begin. She pushed her hair in back of her ears. After a moment, she started. "Collectors have existed for as far back as we have records. Antiquities collectors have probably helped the archaeology world more than their share of times by financing a dig and helping to make sure the finds end up in proper museums, where anyone can study them. But collectors can be just as damaging. By being willing to buy items illegitimately taken from digs, at prices high enough to ensure secrecy, they finance a black market that's very unhealthy for those of us interested in spreading the knowledge we get from our research." She held her glass between her flattened hands and rolled it back and forth.

My drink came at that moment. Based on the length of her preamble, I ordered another. "Don't you get a lot of intangible rewards, though? I mean you learn things from what you find that no one can take away.''

"Of course. But if pot-hunters dig with road-building equipment to grab what they can, they destroy the stratigraphy. And often it's useful to have the actual artifact to study.

Suppose someone had hidden away the Rosetta Stone or the
Timkin Plaque and never let anyone else see it?''

"I don't know about them, but I think I get the point. So
what's the basic problem? We can get to the details later.''

"Artifacts are disappearing from our dig and showing up in
the black market here in town.''

I took a sip from my drink as I considered that. "Maybe
you need a security team. That's not necessarily a job for a
private investigator.'' I hated saying that, but it was true.

"We have a security team. I'm calling at the request of
Sam Lund, the team leader. Those artifacts are disappearing
from a locked, guarded, supposedly impregnable vault.''

"I suppose you're using 'impregnable' in the sense that it's
real difficult to break into,'' I said.

"Yes.''

"I thought you probably were.''

Kate Dunlet leaned back in her chair. "So. Are you ready
for the background?''

"Yeah, but not here. I've got an idea. How about if we
take all the money I've saved for retirement and squander it
on dinner?''

IV.
Will You Take the Case?

For a while, I wondered if I might not be better off really
having to beat up a Womper. Maybe I'm a little precognitive.

Kate and I found a discreet table at Rajalto's, back in a
maze of tiny, irregular booths. She turned off the house music
and I turned down the thermostat.

At odd angles, almost everywhere you looked, were hung
large square mirrors and square panes of glass. There was a
weak resemblance to a fun house, but all the reflecting and
transmitting surfaces were darkened so the overall effect was
muted. The tabletop must have been a half-mirror, because I
could see Kate's tan slacks through the surface as well as the
inverted image of her face.

Thanks to the tricks they played with mirrors, the other faces in the reflections could just as easily have been showing people a hundred meters away rather than right next to us.

"What will you have?" I asked her. At the same moment I pressed the switch that turned on the menus. The tabletop surfaces in front of us turned opaque and showed us the choices available. This was a classy place; only two sections opaqued, so the table mechanism must have figured out there was no one seated at the open side of the table.

I reached over and wiggled my hand in the general area that a third person would have occupied. Another menu section of tabletop opaqued. I took my hand away and that section of the surface turned clear once again.

When I glanced at Kate, she was looking at me with an amused expression.

"Just testing," I said. "In my business, you never know what little tidbits of information might save your life."

"Is that so?" The corners of her mouth turned up a tiny bit more. The doubt in her voice was transparent.

"Maybe we should order," I said. We did.

"You know," I said, ignoring my own recent deficiency, "I'm still surprised at how bad a liar you are. Most people get plenty of practice. And surely being with a university should keep you in good shape."

"What's that supposed to mean?" When she frowned, the overhead light made the faint creases on her forehead more prominent.

"Oh, I'm not picking on your school. I just had the idea that schools were pretty much the same as corporations. I worked in one for a while. At least in my current line of work, the pay is *better* when someone lies."

"Rough place, huh?"

"I had to carry a snake-bite kit *and* kicton-repellent."

"Oh, come on." Kate's eyes reflected the light as she shook her head and grinned. Images of her hair shifted in at least six mirrors.

"I'm serious. They actually employed lawyers. Can you imagine?"

"I'm having trouble making up my mind about whether you're serious."

"Deadly serious. They even had some criminal lawyers."

"So do lots of corporations."

"Not ones like these. With them, the phrase 'criminal lawyer' was redundant."

Kate smiled. "I think that dinner had better arrive soon. I've had enough to drink that it sounds as though you're making sense."

"How about if *you* talk? That way, you don't have to judge."

"OK. Where were we—oh, yes. I can show you the vault. It's out near the dig. It's a walk-in, probably ten meters on a side. Sure, someone could bust a hole through it. But no one could patch it so it didn't show."

"What kinds of things are stolen?"

"Small things—things that would fit in a pocket. But we scan everyone coming out of the dig, so nothing comes out that doesn't go into the vault. In the vault, tagged items that were too dirty when they were excavated get cleaned and formally inventoried."

"But they *are* being stolen?"

"Right. At least two items have shown up in town. They're unmistakably from the right time period and culture. That means our site. Unless there is another site or an old family hoard. And we don't have any evidence to support either of those theories."

Our food arrived, and I considered what she had told me so far. Finally I said, "Aside from wanting to test my honesty, why didn't you just call me out there to look it over right then? And why you instead of security?"

It took her a moment to finish a bite of bread. "Because they're worried. They don't want any overt contact with you. If someone is as good as our thief must be, he could just stop for a while. If you take the case, we'll hire you as an archaeologist. That gives you a good reason to tour the site and be there whenever you need to be."

"That might be a little obvious to the other archaeologists, don't you think? I mean I can dance as fast as anyone I know, but when it comes to fooling someone with years of training, I'll be as useless as sonar in space."

"We could let them in on it. If we can't trust them, we could be out of business anyway. So. What do you think?"

"I think I've got a better idea. Maybe while I'm at this I can give you some lying lessons. Lesson one: stick as close to the truth as you can. Hire me as a specialist. Someone who can help the archaeologists understand inscriptions and things like that, if they find any. I'm pretty good with puzzles. And that still gives me leeway on where and when I go.''

''You're on.''

V.
Do I Have
To Tell You Everything?

Outside the restaurant, the sun made it seem as though we had been in there for only a minute or two. Living in Dallad still gave me that sense of timelessness, as though I were locked in some recurring scene, caught in the land of perpetual early afternoon. The sun was a fixed, unblinking eye. The shadows never grew or shrank a millimeter, as if time waited for all men. Peter Pan would have loved it.

With the help of my wristcomp, I convinced myself that despite appearances it was late in the evening.

''So,'' Kate said. ''I'll meet you tomorrow, and we'll go out to the site?''

''Right,'' I said.

''Thanks, Mr. Takent.''

''It's Ben.''

''Ben,'' she repeated. ''Until then,'' she said, turning to leave.

I stopped her for a moment with one last question. ''There's still something puzzling me about all of this. When you called me with that story about roughing someone up and I indicated that I'd be willing, why didn't you just hang up and try someone else?''

Kate gave me her smile again, the corners of her lips moving up just enough to make me want to grin back at her. ''Maybe I was thirsty, too?''

2

Return to the Scene
Of the Crime

I.

Don't Call Me.
I'll Call You.

The next morning, before meeting Kate Dunlet, I stopped by my office. Odds were I wouldn't be around when the heat-exchanger people came, so I locked everything of value in a secure cabinet and left the front door unlocked. I should have asked Berto how he got in here, but I didn't want to be disillusioned about the sanctity of my office. I didn't lock up a small poster that a past client had given me, the one that said, "No man is an island, but there are still a few peninsulas around." If I were lucky, someone would steal it.

I called the repair people to tell them what I had done. I was about to leave when I looked at my desk screen long enough to realize there was a message waiting. Someone named Morgan wanted me to call. I called, wondering what the subject was, and got a recording saying Morgan was unavailable and to please leave a message. Much as I disliked it, I did.

Maybe I should buy stock in a communications outfit. Then I could be delighted about all the wasted calls and the people who felt the need to avoid doing their unpleasant jobs in person. My mother had called me from a kilometer away to tell me my father had died.

II.

More to It
Than Meets the Eye

The sun was just as hot during the business hours as it had been last night, but I felt a little better as I walked to meet Kate Dunlet. I had slept well, because at least my home heat-exchanger was still working. Maybe I should buy stock in the cooler-repair business.

Humans might be at a disadvantage when it came to heat on the worlds shared by multiple races, but on Tankur at least we had come out lucky by having the clock convenient for us.

We had liked a twenty-four-hour clock ever since we had sundials. Ventons had originated on a world with a twenty-hour rotation. Derjons preferred thirty-two and a half. I didn't know what Wompers liked. I hadn't met one yet who was willing to criticize the status quo of whatever planet was home. On Tankur, since there was no arbitrary standard to conform to, twenty-four was picked as a good compromise.

Unfortunately, even having local time conveniently scaled for us wasn't enough. Tankur's almost perfectly circular orbit eliminates even the smallest synchronizers for body clocks. Tankur provides no daily cycles of temperature, brightness, humidity, or pressure. Not even an electromagnetic field rhythm. Newcomers to Dallad always fall victim to space-lag— Transient Internal Desynchronization as the physiologists like to talk.

The biggest problem is that, with no good cues to help the body resync all its circadian rhythms, TID isn't transient here. In Dallad, it's a way of life.

I was on time, but Kate Dunlet was already there when I reached the parking lot. She had a university skimmer cooled to a comfortable temperature. I climbed in beside her.

"That feels better," I said as the air streamed over me. "Maybe I should concentrate on investigating skimmer thefts or traffic violators."

"It's at least as hot at the site as it is in town. You want

out?'' Kate said it casually, but she still wasn't very good at
deception. She looked studiously at the road rather than force
the point by looking at me. I had the strong feeling she didn't
want me to back out.

"No. I'm fine. Just a little temporary insanity. What's
first?"

Looking forward and smiling, Kate stepped on the acceler-
ator and pulled out of the lot as she said, "I'll show you the
installation, the same tour any first-timer gets. Sam Lund
might want to talk to you if we can make it inconspicuous. He's
the head of security, the one who asked me to call you in."

"He asked for a private eye, or for me in particular?"

"You. Why, you know him?"

"Nope."

Three blocks later, Kate turned onto the main east-west
thoroughfare through Dallad. Twelve lanes stretched out in
each direction, and a three-lane access road lay on either side.
Above the twelve main lanes was another tier of eight more.
There were probably a total of thirty other skimmers in sight.
The city designers had gone a little crazy in worrying about
what might happen to Dallad if it grew the way resort cities
on other planets grew. But so far Dallad had less than half a
million in population, and lots of the residents worked near
their homes, walking when they needed to travel.

The dig was away from the sun, and we had started from
that side of Dallad, so it wasn't long before the city was
behind us and we were on a level plain that had been old even
before humans began to lie about their ages. Kate accelerated.

I hadn't traveled much outside the city since I arrived on
Tankur about two years ago. It was a nice feeling. Tankur
was far from the most highly populated region of space, a
small planet, but quite dense. We were going to travel far
enough that the sun would seem to move in the sky. It was
like traveling from early afternoon to midafternoon. Just an
hour away. If we moved in the opposite direction, we would
reach a place where it was high noon for eternity. Tankur
could have been built there, but it was too dusty thanks to the
winds from each direction that converged there.

Ahead of us and moving slowly toward the road was a dust
devil. They weren't all that common this far from the edge of
night. The twister wasn't quite large enough to be opaque.

Wind buffeted our skimmer briefly as we cut through it, but when I looked back it was continuing on its way, stolidly churning up more dust, unaffected by our passage.

The road cut through gentle rises as though etched with a laser. In the distance ahead, the road seemed as level as the water surface in a calm canal would have been, meeting the horizon and always visible for the same distance. I bet that if I got out of the skimmer at any random place and set a ball bearing on the road's surface, it would stay exactly where it was without the slightest urge to roll in any direction.

Sand and rocks and little hills were almost the only scenery. The few plants that survived on Tankur all grew low enough to the ground that from a distance most of them looked like rocks.

After a while the landscape became boring, so I turned my detecting abilities on Kate Dunlet. She was a relaxed driver, and she must like soft colors a lot. Today her blouse was beige with widely spaced brown stripes. She looked happy. It's incredible how much information a trained sleuth can deduce in a short time.

"How many people work out here?" I asked at last. The skimmer was totally quiet except for the sound of the air rushing past.

"Several hundred. About a hundred archaeologists and other specialists, almost all human, some administrators, a security team, and most of the rest are temporary. Just for this job."

"A hundred archaeologists. That sounds like a lot. Why are they mostly human?"

"It seems humans are more inclined toward archaeology than the other races are. Not much exploration had been done before we first reached the stars. You probably know how tenuous life seems to be. What we mostly found at first was either the rubble left by long-since-destroyed civilizations or the embryos of new ones millions of years from being sentient. No one before us had been very interested in the rubble. And there's lots of it. If a race manages to survive until the 100-century mark, they probably spend the first ninety-nine centuries before their weapons outpace their judgment."

Far ahead, the horizon was losing its flatness. Until this point, the only significant landmark had been a stalled skimmer.

"It was probably overwhelming for a while," Kate continued. "There were more things to study than there were trained people. But we're finally starting to catch up."

"But you must be fairly good to get to do this while you're still young," I said.

"I like to think that." She smiled and then grew serious. "Do you need to change your name or anything like that?"

"I don't think so. Only lie about what you have to."

The horizon had grown rougher by the time we neared the site, and it seemed to be midafternoon. I actually had a sense of time moving again. Being there was a pleasant change from the flat city. A little farther to the west was a large reddish-brown butte, probably a kilometer wide, poking up from the desert a hundred meters or more. On either side of it in the distance lay the edge of a large mesa.

"How did you ever know to start digging here?" I asked as she pulled up in front of a long trailer topped with solar panels.

"A Derjon family was on a hiking trip. They found what looked like a portion of a brick, and they brought it to the authorities. Not long after that, the university established a branch here."

"A brick doesn't sound all that special."

"I guess it's a question of where you find it. If you find something like that where it has no right to be, it gets your curiosity going. You know?"

"Yeah."

"So. You ready to go inside?"

"No. I think I forgot my magnifying glass."

In answer, she opened her door. I followed her. After the frigid air in the skimmer, the warmth felt good as we walked to an enormous trailer resting on the ground. The sign on the door identified the building as an extension of the University of Alteson. They don't build schools like they used to.

The interior of the trailer looked better than the outside. The door, despite its faded exterior, sealed tightly against the frame as I pulled it closed. Inside there was the steady hiss of forced air.

Near the door was a small terminal on a desk. Kate had me put my thumb on the attached panel as she entered the authorization for my name to be added to the access list.

Great. Now still another source would probably start sending me advertising messages.

Rows of desks occupied most of the space next to the walls. On the walls themselves were numerous holograms of the site and individual artifacts.

Once we were finished, Kate said, "Come on back this way. There should be someone around." She led me down a narrow central hallway flanked by closed doors at regular intervals until we came onto a large area with several desks all unoccupied.

"That's funny," she said. "There's almost always someone here. Oh well. It's probably better this way anyway. I can show you the chart room to get you oriented."

She opened a nearby door and preceded me into what looked to be a totally empty square room. At intervals around the room were small circular holes. Holes in the same style formed a rectangular grid on the ceiling. I had a feeling for what was coming, but not the thoroughness or quality.

Kate shut the door and went to stand in the center of the room. She clapped her hands and a holographic menu sprang into the air directly in front of her. She pushed her hand through the letters forming the words "Full Top View."

Even being prepared for it wasn't enough to stop me from taking a deep appreciative breath as the lights went out and the room flooded with the most highly detailed hologram I could remember seeing. Spreading out level at knee height was an intricate representation of the surrounding several square kilometers. Across the room, the nearby butte rose a quarter of the way to the ceiling. I walked closer to the center. As I did, the area behind me filled in, as though I were a ghost walking through a pool of iridescent water.

"That's Vandict Butte next to the site," Kate said. "Barteem Mesa is beyond it."

From above, the Vandict Butte top was flat and nearly square. At one wall, the edge of the mesa rose to about the same height as the butte. Individual rocks and outcroppings were so detailed that their shadows showed.

"Site boundary," Kate said a little more loudly than necessary for normal conversation, and an irregular ring began to glow red not far from the edge of the butte. Outside the

circle, I could see a tiny rectangle which had to be the trailer
we were presently in.

"Could you blow it up a little?" I asked. "I can't remember if I closed the door."

"Cute," Kate said. "But this isn't live. It's all in the
database." Then, certainly trying to impress me even more,
she put it through some exercise. The scale of the image
started to expand so realistically I felt a twinge of acrophobia
as we seemed to fall toward the plain below. Moments later,
it was as though we had just landed outside the trailer and its
image filled most of the room.

From there, we took a high-speed cruise toward the site. A
few times it really looked like we were going to smash
ourselves into one obstruction or another. Small outbuildings
flashed past until the security perimeter showed ahead. Tall
poles, perhaps ten meters high, set at ten-meter intervals,
ringed the site. In place around a third of the circle were
transparent dust guards. And then we were airborne again,
rising quickly enough that I inhaled reflexively. When we had
risen to the point where the red circle below filled about a
quarter of the room, Kate turned on yellow iso-elevation lines.

"The site's a gentle cone," Kate said. She walked to the
center of the circle, where the concentric lines showed a
gradual rise. "The center is only a meter higher than the
perimeter, but it's quite deliberate.

"You want to see what it used to look like?" she asked,
and, without waiting for an answer, she gave another command. As we watched, the circle of the site gradually flattened out as holes filled in and the ring of perimeter poles
vanished. We were left looking at what seemed to be virgin
desert. Kate spoke another command and the process reversed, showing the growth of the site, and this time I noticed
the outbuildings springing into existence.

She gave a few more commands, and then zoomed back
toward the ground, continuing until the image was apparently
several times life size. Superimposed on the scene was a
rectangular grid of reference lines. When the magnification
settled, in front of us lay a surprisingly well-preserved bowl
with a surviving pattern of circles and squares. Above the
bowl hung a blue coded description which doubtless would
give additional details on the bowl itself.

"That's the exact place that bowl was found," Kate said. "Here's what else was there." The bowl vanished, and several shards of another artifact lay on the ground. "And here's what the bowl looks like by itself." Instantly, the bowl hung right-side-up in the air and began to rotate slowly, showing a crack on the opposite side. Then the normal color image was replaced by a color-coded image on which a yellow crack stood out sharply from the rest of the predominantly blue image.

She gave the projection another command, and the nearby loose shards began to move. They came together into the composite box as though an exploding box had been recorded in reverse action.

Kate clapped her hands and the scene vanished, replaced by the vacant walls of the room. "So. What do you think?"

"I'm impressed. And curious. The pattern on the box, the waves with small circles interspersed. That reminds me of patterns I've seen in Womper art."

She slowly turned to look at me. "Go on."

"I'm not sure where I was going. I guess I was just wondering if this might have been where they originated."

"Some of us are wondering that very thing. But there's not enough evidence to say that conclusively yet."

"Can you bring up the display one more time? I'd like to see your impregnable vault. And how it fits into the surroundings."

She did. The vault looked solid. It sat outside the red circle, on a level area in plain view from most of the site. The building was square with thick-looking walls and a door that would have looked at home in a bank. Next to the door was a small, cooled booth large enough to keep a guard comfortable.

"That's enough," I said after a few moments' thought. "I think it's time we actually walked around." As we were on our way out, I said, "Do you have any idea how handy that setup could be for keeping track of my collection of bad debts?"

III.
Don't Look Now

Outside the trailer, it was again midafternoon, even though it was actually before noon according to my wristcomp. Kate and I walked along a sandy path toward the site. I felt like I had already seen some of the individual pebbles along the way. Small green and brown plants showed just enough for them to gather a little direct sunlight.

About the only thing I wasn't actually prepared for was the actual size of the encircled dig. "It's smaller than I thought it was," I said as we reached the point where the entire ring of perimeter guard poles were in sight.

"I know," Kate said. "That's one of the puzzles. Early villages might be this small, but usually not cities. Yet some of the construction is a lot more sophisticated than we associate with villages."

"*One* of the puzzles?" I said.

"We've got several more. For instance, why here? Why not nearer the edge of night where water wells don't have to be so deep? Everything we have to go on indicates that Tankur stopped having traveling days and nights long before this village existed. Dallad was built where it was because we knew enough about the water table to trust it. For another thing, initial measurements indicate this site had an active lifetime of no more than a couple of centuries. Why did it die? And their tools—" Kate broke off as a man appeared on the trail ahead of us.

"Dr. Fenton," Kate said once he was close. "I want you to meet Ben Takent. He's come out to help us analyze some of the finds."

"Quite. Glad to have you aboard," Fenton said stiffly, as though he already knew why I was really here and wished there were an alternative. He was middle-aged, with a deeper tan than Kate. He seemed to be chewing something, but my guess was that it was just a habit. Kate explained that Fenton was the senior archaeologist on site.

"What have you found out so far?" Fenton asked me. He had to have known I just got there.

"I think it was done with mirrors. You see, they set a holographic copy of the vault, and then they—"

Fenton wasn't slow. His irritation began to show well before I stopped. "Sorry," I said. "It's way too early for me to have found out anything, and I haven't. Do you want a refund?" Maybe that's why I get along better with non-humans—non-humans don't let my sense of humor get to them as much.

Fenton's lips pressed together, and he shook his head with a barely discernible motion. He left without saying anything more, heading back for the trailer.

Kate looked at me for a moment, and then we resumed our walk. We could have gone immediately to the vault but decided it would be more natural to see the actual dig first.

"Are you usually this easy to get along with?" Kate asked.

I wiped my forehead. "No. Just while the sun's out."

Most of the activity at the site was concentrated in the enclosed circle. Numerous small groups spread across the irregular ground. Half the people I could see wore silvery hot-weather clothes, glittering brightly as they moved. By the time we reached the guard shack just outside the circle, we could see the tops of exposed walls that had been excavated.

"Hello, Elliot," Kate said to the guard who came out of the shack to meet us. She introduced him as Elliot Pardo.

If he was any indication of the normal security team member, they didn't rely solely on the optical fence posts. I wouldn't want to meet Elliot with an artifact in my back pocket. I said "hello" politely.

Elliot was slightly taller than me. And slightly more muscular. He probably hadn't had his exercise curtailed lately by spending half his waking hours in the heat. "You're new," Elliot said. "We haven't gotten many new folks lately." He gave me the sign-in log and a frank, appraising glance. His eyebrows were so bushy they might help keep the sun out of his eyes.

I put my signature on the log while Kate gave him the cover story. Sam Lund, the security team leader was the only security person who knew about me. I meant to ask him if that implied he suspected some of his subordinates.

Elliot's biceps flexed as he took the log back from me. I was sure he deliberately squeezed the log to show off. He entered a command at the console in his shack and waved us through. Just across the line between the two posts, there was another shack, along with some scanning equipment that looked powerful enough to be a serious invasion of privacy.

The inside guard was Rummel Hurdt, a smiling Venton. His shack stood open, the heat-exchanger obviously shut off. Rummel sat comfortably on a stool shaded by the shack. Kate performed the introductions again.

"Nice day," I said.

Rummel grinned at me, his canines sparkling white. "This is one planet where even the late shift is good." His dark eyes against his untanned face gave the impression of two black marbles dropped into snow.

I wiped my forehead. Snow would be nice. "Think it will rain today?" I asked.

Rummel made a show of sweeping the horizon, looking for nonexistent clouds. "My guess is no," he said.

"I suppose you're right." This far from the edge of night, occasional rains were months apart.

We left Rummel sitting in comfort and strolled along in the heat. Inside the circle, we had to be more careful where we walked. The main paths were well marked with tiny flags. Jutting out of the ground nearby was a firmly anchored post with a shiny globe on top. Kate confirmed that it was part of the coordinate reference system. All over the site were neat piles of dirt next to recently dug cavities.

The first person we came across as we walked was a Womper. Kate stopped and introduced us. "Ben Takent, Zeldon Tal."

Zeldon shook my hand, his massive fist making me feel like a child shaking hands with an adult even though my hand wasn't that small. When a Womper shook hands with you, he really *shook* your hand.

Kate gave him the cover story, and he said, "So you may be able to help us unlock mysteries, Mr. Takent?" Zeldon was about my height but probably massed about three times what I did. By human standards, Zeldon had an incredible case of equatorial bulge. His face was almost perfectly round. He had no hair on his head at all, not even eyebrows. His eyes were so large they reminded me of sad-eyed human caricatures. By Womper standards, he was a trim, good-looking guy.

"To early to tell," I said. "Can you tell me what you're doing there, though?"

"Dating," Zeldon said.

"Excuse me? I'm already spoken for."

"Determining the date that the items you see here were buried. Without some of the easy clues available on other planets, such as glaciers and tree rings, it's a difficult task. We are using microfossil evolution and some more exotic techniques."

This was as clear to me as the reason yawns are catching. "I see," I said.

Zeldon blinked his large eyes at me.

"Let's go see what's drawing the crowd," Kate said, pointing toward the largest group we could see. "See you later, Zeldon."

The gathering included a few more Wompers, a couple of Ventons, but most of the rest were humans. As we walked, we passed a series of low walls, most of which were about ten centimeters wide. Nearby, a woman was using a sonic vibrator to clear dust from an object I couldn't see clearly.

Most of the people in the small crowd ahead paid us little attention as we approached, but a woman wearing a green pullover shirt and gray shorts moved toward us.

"Who's your friend, Kate?" she asked, smiling. Kate introduced me to Allison Vivono, yet another archaeologist. Allison looked just a little older than Kate.

"What's the excitement?" Kate asked her after the exchange.

"It looks as if we've come across a burial ground. We'll know for sure in a few minutes."

Kate gave Allison a wide-eyed look which I interpreted to mean that burial sites yielded more information about former residents than some other kinds of discoveries might. Allison confirmed that for me as she combed her black hair into place with her fingers. She went on and on about how you could determine age at death, cause of death, and burial customs just from the bones. If they could find enough skeletons, they could generate demographics.

I tuned out just a little as she kept on talking. In my business, if the bones were more than a few years old, they weren't much good to anyone.

While we were talking, a man and a woman near the center

of the group finished erecting a rectangular structure on the ground. Together, they then took a square black box from its case and suspended the box between two long, parallel strips. The woman kneeled beside the box and punched in some commands on a panel on top of it.

She stepped back, and a moment later the box began to move. Supported by the two strips, the box slowly traveled level over the ground for a distance of more than a meter. It stopped and beeped softly.

There was a mass movement toward a nearby crate that looked like a short, open coffin. The "ooh" and "ah" crowd gave it high praise.

Finally, we were able to get close enough to get a glimpse of what was in the crate. It was a hologram, obviously displaying what the scanner had detected beneath the dirt. Near the top were several well-defined objects including a knife, a small cube, and what was likely a necklace. Markings on the cube looked like a square and two adjacent smaller circles. Inside the square lay an equilateral triangle. Next to the cube was a flat plate with an inscribed triangle surrounding the spiral Womper symbol for birth.

Progressively deeper in the hologram, objects were less well defined, but near the bottom were what could only be a pair of hands, as though the body had been deeply buried on its back, in a sleep-walking posture. The thick bones reminded me of a decomposed Womper body I had been unfortunate enough to see. Kate hold me that whenever possible they dig feet first to avoid damaging the skull.

At each corner of the hologram were X, Y, and Z coordinates that I was sure were tied into their master file of the site. Very thorough.

As I stood there thinking every minute that went by made it seem more difficult to steal from this place, someone came up behind me silently. Whoever it was did nothing more than say quietly enough for only me to hear, "Meet me in the front trailer in twenty minutes." His voice was scratchy.

I cleared my throat and nodded slightly as though responding to something one of the people nearer the coffin had said. After I heard four or five receding steps, I wiped more sweat from my forehead and used the motion to get a glimpse of a man with a white explorer's hat with a black star on the back of it. I waited a few more minutes before I stepped forward and said to Kate, "You want to give me the rest of the tour?"

She looked at me and then back at the display in the coffin and said, "Sure. Anything in particular?"

"One thing I'm interested in is the exact center of the site, the highest elevation point," I said, loud enough for others to hear.

"Let's go."

We had traveled far enough from the group to avoid being overheard when I casually pointed toward our destination and said, "Look where I'm pointing while I ask you a question. Don't look anywhere else."

"Right," she said, picking up quickly.

I described the man who had spoken to me. "I'm going to stumble in just a minute. When you help me up, try to look around and see if you can tell me who he is."

I took a couple more steps and caught my foot on an imaginary obstruction, stumbling just enough to lose my balance without actually falling flat on my face. Maybe I was in the wrong profession. Maybe I should have been an actor. Probably their heat-exchangers worked all the time.

Kate's hand on my arm helped me as I recovered. She left it there longer than necessary as she looked surreptitiously around. "I can't tell," she said. "It's got to be someone on the security team, but that's all I know."

She finally realized she was still holding my arm and let go of it and gave me a wry grin. I grinned back.

"What makes you think there's anything special about the center?" she asked abruptly.

"There's bound to be something if this is really an ancient Womper village. Circles and squares figure heavily in their main religion. Their holy buildings are usually round. And all the important activities take place in the center of the building. But that's beside the point."

"That same thought has occurred to several of us. You might make a good archaeologist. But still, all that doesn't necessarily mean they buried things there a hundred centuries ago, and what exactly is the point then?"

I told her about the message. "I guess what this means is there are two possibilities. One, that man was your security

team leader, Sam Lund. Or two, someone who's not supposed to know who I am or why I'm really here may know
more than he's authorized to.''

"No one else could know.''

"OK. Then it had to be Sam Lund.''

3

I Love a Mystery

I.

One Picture Is Worth A Thousand Words

Kate and I walked back to the perimeter guard shack. Rummel Hurdt was just as courteous and friendly as before, but, when he asked us to go through the scanner to make sure we weren't carrying anything out, I was sure he'd put up a good fight before taking "no" for an answer.

Rummel smiled at us, revealing his large canines again. He looked at ease, sitting in the heat and holding a cool red drink in a transparent, insulated container. But the weapon on his hip looked businesslike.

I felt nothing as I followed Kate through the scanner. The scanner itself was outwardly just a two-meter-tall communications booth but with doors on opposite sides. And no communications panel.

"Mr. Takent," Rummel said after I went through. His tone of voice suggested a problem in the making as he looked at the display the scanner had generated in his guard shack.

"Yes?" I said, positive that I hadn't absent-mindedly put a rock in my pocket.

"You really should get some more ink in your pen soon. You're almost out."

31

I grinned as I pulled an old pen out of my shirt pocket. I casually hefted it in my hand and said, "You're right. I can't imagine how I let it go this long."

Rummel grinned back at me. "And your pants are missing a snap on the back left pocket."

"I already know all this stuff about me, you know. Why don't you tell me about her?" I gestured at Kate. "Can I get a couple of eight-by-tens and a wallet-size?"

"Would you two stop it?" Kate said good-naturedly.

"It's OK," Rummel said to me. "I couldn't do that anyway. Have a little respect for a person's privacy." He took a quick last took at his display before winking one dark eye at me. "You know you really should chew your breakfast more thoroughly."

We started to leave, but I turned back with one last question. "What do you do with your picture collection?"

"It's archived. *Everything* around here is archived."

Rummel signaled to Elliot that we were coming through. I couldn't see anything change, but Elliot motioned us to come ahead.

Elliot looked annoyed with me for staying so long on the other side.

We began walking toward the trailer. Once we passed out of Elliot's hearing, I said to Kate, "Sure seems like a lot of precautions. What happens if someone just throws an artifact out over the tops of the perimeter poles?"

"An alarm goes off. And the trajectory is plotted, along with the calculated landing point."

"That sounds more appropriate for a planetary defense system. You really take this seriously, don't you?"

"We think it's reasonable. Depending on the artifact's scarcity, you could put several years' salary into a pocket without making it bulge."

"Is that a gun in your pocket or are you just—"

"What?" Kate said.

"Nothing."

There was no one in the lobby of the trailer, but as we walked along the corridor, a door opened abruptly, and a man motioned us inside one of the rooms.

"Ben Takent, Sam Lund," Kate said as Sam closed the door.

When he spoke, I was sure Sam was the person who had whispered to me back at the dig. "What have you found out so far?" he asked me. His voice was scratchy, as though he needed to clear his throat. It made me want to clear mine.

"Well, there were these mirrors, see—" I started and then broke off. "Nothing actually. I haven't had much time to absorb it all yet."

"He's half right, Sam," Kate said. "Maybe he doesn't know how the artifacts are disappearing, but he realized this is probably an old Womper village on the basis of lot less information than we had, and *before* he saw that Womper skeleton out there."

Sam looked at me. His black hair was combed straight back from his forehead. He looked like a bald man who had started a hair restoration job but hadn't finished yet. Sam was probably twenty years my senior, but he projected an image that said he still had the energy to do whatever was necessary to finish the job.

"I'm glad you're here, Mr. Takent," Sam said. "This calls for a bit more subtlety than a security team can handle. I haven't told any of my people about you. You have any questions Kate hasn't answered yet?"

I thought about a couple of interesting questions for Kate. "No. She's answered everything I've asked."

"If anything comes up, you can ask Kate to ask me, so we don't attract attention."

"Sounds good. But now that I think about it, I do have a question for you. Does the fact that you haven't told your team about me mean you suspect them or that you're just a bad conversationalist?"

"Those are all good people, Mr. Takent—"

"Ben."

"Ben. We run them through a lot of tests. It would be hard for them to fake the results. I can't bring myself to believe one of them is responsible."

"But."

Sam hesitated. "But I have to be careful. Elliot Pardo's been talking in private about coming into some money lately. I can't take a chance on being wrong." He swept his hand straight back, pushing his hair flat against his scalp.

"Just how do you know that?"

"I hear everything that goes on here if it's transmitted on a wristcomp or said within ten meters of any guard shack."

"Sounds like a person gives up a lot of privacy to work here," I said.

"You might say that."

"I did say that. One more question: who controls the gate—the inside guard or the outside guard?"

"The outside. The one inside does a scan and reports to the outside. If there's anything strange in the scan, whoever it is stays inside until it's normal."

"And does the perimeter have any weaponry, or is it just detection?"

"Detection only. You can walk out anywhere. But you can't do it without the world knowing about it."

"Has anyone ever walked out?"

"Never."

"Never is a long time. I think I'd better have a look at the vault."

II.

Stone Walls Do Not
A Prison Make

The vault looked as impregnable as Kate had described it. I leaned on the one wall that held shade, pretending that getting out of the sun was my real purpose. It was like leaning against a safe in a casino.

"I think the moat must have dried up in the heat," I said.

"The inside is a little cooler," Kate said.

We walked around front to the guard shack. This guard's name was Maxwell, and she seemed every bit as cautious as Rummel and Elliot had been. After checking our identifications, she let us in single file, first Kate and then me. The outer door could have passed the test for submarine use on a heavy-gravity planet.

Once I was through the door and it thudded solidly closed

behind me, a similar door opened in front of me, and I saw at my sides the same kind of sensors that had been used in the scanning booth at the dig.

Kate was waiting for me inside. Beyond her lay rows of shelves and drawers. I didn't look at any of the items recovered from the dig at first. I started walking around the perimeter of the vault, looking carefully at the walls, the seams between walls and ceiling, and the base of each wall. "It's hotter in here than I expected," I said.

"It's not meant primarily for human comfort," Kate said. "It's designed to protect the contents and to be tolerable for us."

In one corner of the vault there were two people busily working near a sink.

"What goes on there?" I asked Kate.

"They're cleaning some of the smaller items so they can be officially catalogued. Some five thousand years ago the water table rose dramatically and then fell again. When you add water to the mix of elements in this dirt and sand, you can sometimes get fairly solid encrustation on pieces. Those items are brought here with all the other finds, and they're cleaned before they're fully catalogued."

I walked closer to the two as they worked. Neither seemed interested in introductions, so I backed away. Before I did, though, I noticed an encrusted artifact that seemed to me to be precariously balanced near the edge of the work table.

"You know," I said to Kate, "With stuff this valuable, I'm surprised that—"

There came a crash from the general area of the work table, and pieces of artifact and rock scattered across the floor.

Kate frowned and looked back toward the work area as one of the cleaners began to pick up the pieces. "What?" she said, not looking at me.

"Never mind." I resumed my inspection.

I felt the wall that was on the sun side and then felt the wall opposite. They both seemed to be about the same temperature. I jumped up and down on the floor at several points and looked for seams in the floor. It was hard to even find scratches. As Kate watched me, her quizzical expression said surely there had to be more advanced techniques than this.

The shelves and cabinets were the rolling kind so there

were only two actual aisles at a time, and they could be relocated. I rolled the shelves and made sure I looked at every square meter of floor space.

Once I was finished with the main things I was interested in, I spent a few minutes looking at the items lining the shelves. One knife looked to my eye as though it had been machined. Tiny parallel grooves gave the surface a burnished appearance. Below the knife was a long number.

"And where are the newest items kept when they're fully catalogued?" I asked.

Kate showed me the most recent three shelves. The items on the shelves ranged from a necklace to a mostly whole cup. The broken edge of the cup looked more like someone had laser-cut a piece of aluminum than it looked like a damaged piece of pottery. Each item had a red, numbered sticker and a printed tag on a string tied to it.

"These are the two items we know of that showed up in town," Kate said. "One of the other archaeologists spotted them down on East Market at the place called Bertram's. When he bought the pieces, the owner wouldn't say how he had acquired them."

I looked closely at them. There was a knife and a decorated box. They certainly looked to me to be consistent with the other artifacts that had been excavated.

"Ah hah," I said at last.

" 'Ah hah' what?" Kate asked.

"Not here. Let's talk outside."

Once we were out past the airlock scanner and in the bright sunshine, Kate again said, " 'Ah hah' what?"

"Let's talk in your skimmer with the cooler on."

She was obviously impatient, but I didn't want to talk in the open.

In the skimmer with a stream of cold air on my face, I said, "This might be a little harder than I thought."

"Go on."

"Well, if the artifacts were being taken from the vault, then we could establish a surveillance of it, and then—"

"What do you mean *if*?"

"They're not. Or at least I'm fairly sure they're not."

"Sam Lund thinks they are."

"Maybe that's the easiest thing for him to believe. That

doesn't make it necessarily the most likely explanation. It's been my experience that when things seem impossible, they almost always are. It's like magic tricks. The magician directs you to believe in something impossible when what's really happening is possible but concealed by misdirection. Besides, stealing artifacts after they're in the vault is a little like expecting a murderer to pick up a hitchhiker and not kill him until he pulls up in front of a police station.''

Kate sat for a moment, her gray eyes searching mine. "So. What *is* happening?"

"I don't know yet. Maybe someone has found a way to defeat the scanners. But if he has, he could just as easily be stealing from the dig. I think an ordinary two-pronged approach is what I need. One, I mount a good camera somewhere where it can get an unobstructed view of the site. And two, I work backward from the items that were sold in town.'' I was getting comfortable enough so I redirected the vent that had been cooling my face.

"The vault is secure? So you're convinced that's the truth?''

"That's *a* truth. You're not paying me enough for *the truth.*''

III.

Wild Blue Yonder

By midafternoon, what was *really* midafternoon, I was ten kilometers over the dig, flying away from the sun. Kate had dropped me off back in town, and it hadn't taken long to rent some equipment and find a private plane for hire.

"That's it down there," I shouted to the pilot and pointed at Vandict Butte next to the site.

He nodded. It was one of his longest sentences. I had wanted to find someone who wouldn't talk much, but I hadn't thought it all the way through.

We flew far enough that we should be out of sight of the dig before the pilot put the craft into a lazy turn and began to lose altitude. Features on Barteem Mesa below us began to grow. By the time we saw Vandict Butte ahead, we were cruising no more than a hundred meters off the flat mesa top.

"Somewhere in the middle—not near the far side," I said loudly. The pilot nodded again.

There was more turbulence as we crossed the gap between the mesa and the butte, and the pilot flipped a couple of switches. Over the butte, he flipped another couple of switches and began moving the throttle. The roar from outside the cabin grew louder, and I realized the jets were angling toward the ground. The butte looked even flatter than the mesa.

We touched down gently, and I said in a louder voice than necessary, "You're going to wait for me, right?"

The pilot nodded.

"Nice talking to you," I said.

He looked at his wristcomp.

I grabbed the pack behind my seat and opened my door. By the time I had scrambled out and pushed the door closed, the pilot had started his siesta.

The angle of the sun made it simple to know which way I wanted to go. I looked back several times as I made my way across the dusty butte, and each time the aircraft was easy to locate. I was thirsty and hot long before I made it to the edge of the butte.

I walked along the rim, back far enough that I wouldn't be visible to people at the dig, looking for a stable surface near the precipice. When I found one, I crawled forward far enough to see the view below. Below me was a surprisingly long, nearly vertical drop.

I withdrew the rental camera from my pack and secured it with stakes and filament. The drop made me nervous, so I backed up and unfolded the solar panel and plugged it in. I tilted it toward the sun to maximize the output power and to keep dust from settling on it.

With the camera in setup mode, I made it hold a wide-angle view long enough to satisfy me that it could see everything that could possibly be of interest, and then some. From this height and angle, the dig appeared to be an ellipse of pins stuck in the ground below.

I used the camera to scan the dig manually. In a moment, the ellipse filled my wristcomp screen. Swiftly it zoomed toward the rough location of the guard shack until the shack occupied the center ten percent of the screen. I zoomed farther and saw that Rummel was still on duty. At this magnification, the heat shimmers gave his motionless body the illusion of action. That would complicate matters.

Carefully, I gave the camera instructions for a threshold of motion detection. I wanted to capture genuine activity but ignore the apparent motion caused by the heat waves, so I set it to average each ten images. That should counteract at least some of the ripples. I had to set it to a level that might miss small actions while making sure it recorded anything big. Finally, I initiated autoscan.

Perfect. I watched my screen for a minute as the camera began simultaneously recording and transmitting. More quickly than I could follow the image, it began alternating between long shots and various closeups of any motion it detected in its field of view. Each frame was labeled with magnification and coordinates, so I could piece together any thread I wanted to follow later.

For one last double-check, I told my wristcomp to display only those images that fell in one narrow range of angles. On my small screen a second later was a view of two people carefully digging along the base of a short wall. Then I called my office computer and had it relay what it was receiving. Everything looked good. The signal would be automatically routed via whatever communications satellite was nearest at the moment. There was no such thing as a synchronous satellite around Tankur.

I hated to admit it, but this camera was worth its weight in artifacts. It would have been more rewarding to avoid relying on technology, but the camera did the job of more people than I could afford to hire.

I was hot and dusty, impatient to be back in the plane, but I had to pause a moment longer in appreciation of the view. I had been on Tankur so long that sitting up on the butte was a gratifying break from the usual flatness. The ground surrounding the dig was as flat as any near Dallad, but over to my right, nearly even with the other side of the butte, was a small bluff and a long, twisting arroyo. Probably that was fairly typical this near the edge of the butte and the mesa. From this far up, the small plants were nothing more than speckles on the dirt.

I finally got back to my feet, well back from the edge, and started the long walk back to the waiting plane and the pilot with the glib tongue.

IV.

Hot Time
In the Old Town Tonight

It was late by the time I got back to the land of early afternoon, and my office felt hot enough to melt plastic. It even smelled like melted plastic. The heat-exchanger people hadn't left a message saying not to expect them, and they obviously hadn't been there, so I hoped it wouldn't be much longer. At least I had been in comfort for over half of the day.

I stopped by my apartment long enough for a cool shower. I had a small place, just a tiny kitchen, a small bedroom, a bathroom, and a modest living room. There wasn't much of a view; I had a ground-floor apartment on a narrow side street similar to the one my office was on. It suited me and was a lot cheaper than apartments with sun exposure. Light pipes fed sunlight into an indirect trough near the ceiling. It was late enough that my windows had opaqued in a vain effort to help my body synchronize to day and night.

I changed into my fresh clothes in the living room so I could look at some of my paintings.

I had a smattering of art from several cultures, but what currently took up half of my wall space were Womper products. Many of them used circles, squares, and dots as almost the only simple shapes, building the more complex forms from small circles and squares. I didn't understand why if they wanted to use the basic geometrical figures they didn't use any equilateral triangles. And yet the box at the site had been decorated with a triangle.

One painting in particular reminded me so much of the pattern on the vase at the site that it alone would have convinced me that the university was indeed uncovering an unbelievably old Womper community. Wompers lived on about six worlds that I knew of, all in this part of the galaxy. Theory said they had originated on one of the six and migrated with space-faring people to the other worlds, but, since none of those same space-farers were the sticklers for history that humans seemed to be, no one was sure which planet was their starting point.

I got up, thinking there was something more that I should be understanding about all this, and left. It was still hot enough to roast a cockroach outside. Oh, give me a planet where the cliche was, "If you don't like the weather, just wait five minutes." I wouldn't even mind if people had inane conversations about changes in the weather.

I got my skimmer from the lot and drove to another lot near the neighborhood I wanted to visit. I walked along a wide, hot street, wondering why I had bothered to shower.

One of the first bars I passed was a place that catered to Derjons. The building didn't actually glow incandescently, but the fact that they *heated* it gave me the sweats. Several doors down was a more typical bar, one that could suit anyone's requirements. I walked into the brightly lit Sand and Sun.

It was fortunate for the owners that they got their energy from solar panels. The place was a thermodynamicist's dream gone mad. Next to each seat was an adjustable nozzle like the ones on spaceliners. So Derjons, Ventons, and Wompers could sit under a stream of exhaust-pipe air and humans could stick their heads in refrigerators. In a place like this, you never had to worry about air circulation. The music tonight consisted of plaintive twanging sounds, someone's attempt to produce a music that appealed to all four races and succeeded in pleasing none.

I was looking around for a couple of people I knew who could tell me about recent activities on the black market when I saw someone else I knew. Berto.

He saw me at about the same moment. He excused himself from the table where several friends were laughing and talking. Several partly full glasses of red wine littered the table. Or were they partly empty? I never could remember.

"How'd you get in here?" I asked him.

"I don't think anybody but a Venton can tell how old another Venton is. The bartenders here have given up trying, man."

"I can tell how old you are." I grabbed his hand and turned it palm up. His palm was textured with a leathery pattern. As Ventons aged, the squares in the pattern grew smaller.

"You're not just anybody. What are you doing here? You act like you're looking."

"I am. You see Bertillion or Zanderveldt tonight?"

"Nope. What do you need them for?"

I told him a little.

"Why bother with them? Tanto works down there. He could tell you if anyone's selling those artifact things."

"That's Tanto on the far right? The one who just spilled his drink all over himself?"

"That's him."

"Terrific." I started toward a table and stopped. "Talk to him quietly. If he really does know anything about what's going on in the market lately, you two come and see me."

"How much?"

"I'll buy you some drinks."

"That's not much."

"Bertillion and Zanderveldt will be free. They owe me. I'll give you more if I get anything great."

"OK, man." Berto gave me a big grin.

If he had been human, I would have ruffled his hair, but Ventons had thin, sparse hair and the gesture wouldn't have conveyed the same feeling. I punched him lightly on the arm.

I found a seat, turned on the cool air, and ordered a drink. Not much later, Berto and Tanto joined me. My drink arrived seconds afterward.

"We'll have what he's having," Berto said to the waiter, a guy about my age.

"That sounds good," I said. "Two more coffees." I looked hard at the waiter and he nodded.

"Hey, wait a minute—" Berto started.

"No, Berto, I insist. I know you didn't want to have anything fancy and expensive, but I insist. I'd never forgive myself if I let you be so polite that I just ordered you a cheap stimulant. Really. When you treat someone, you have to do it right.'' I nodded once again to the waiter and he went on his way.

Tanto had his lips pressed together in the universal expression of disgust.

I looked at him. ''Just because I want to ask some questions doesn't mean I want to get caught buying for minors. And you'll like the coffee.'' It was true. Most of the adult Ventons I knew liked coffee even better than humans did.

Tanto looked at Berto and said, ''You ready to go?''

''No. Let's try this coffee. And I think you should tell this man what you know anyway. He's a good guy.''

Tanto finally appeared to soften. He could have been Berto's older brother except he didn't brush his teeth often enough. Berto's canines were bright white, even in the bar lighting. Tanto's were flesh colored. And that's not very appealing with canines as pronounced as they are on Ventons.

Their coffee arrived while I was sipping mine. There was just a hint of a smile on the waiter's face as he placed the mugs on the table. I waited until he left before asking my first question. ''Tanto, Berto tells me you know about what goes on in the market. I'm trying to find out about a couple of things—a knife and a small box with a carved lid. They're a little unusual because they have designs like these on them.'' I traced a pattern in the waxy tabletop surface.

Tanto tasted his coffee before he replied. His lips curled just a little at first, but then he took a bigger sip. ''There might be some stuff like that at Bertram's.''

''Bertram's,'' I said, keeping the disappointment out of my voice.

''Yeah. Bertram's. They got lots of stuff like that.''

Bertram's was the place where Kate had told me the two items turned up. I needed to know their route. The fact that Tanto told me so little indicated he wasn't planning to tell me anything of value. ''How's the coffee?'' I asked.

''I'm still making up my mind,'' Berto said. ''Maybe it's OK.''

Tanto leaned back and let his short legs stick into the aisle. ''I'll let you know. I think I've tasted worse.''

Terrific. I kept my eyes open, looking for Bertillion and Zanderveldt. All I saw was a loud drunk five tables away. I leaned back and let the cool air hit my face straight on for a minute.

"Well, thanks for your information, Tanto," I said at last. "I guess I'd better be going."

"Don't go yet, bug eye," Berto said, taking Tanto by the arm. Obviously he, too, knew Tanto wasn't being helpful.

"No. It's OK," I said before Berto said anything else.

I was reaching for my money when the drunk I had noticed earlier tripped on Tanto's outstretched feet. That was really quite an accomplishment, considering how short Tanto's legs were.

I got up and tried to help the drunk to his feet, starting to apologize for Tanto. The guy was human, probably ten years and twenty kilos ahead of me. He didn't want to be helped. In fact, he took a swing at me that I easily dodged.

"Just trying to help, pal," I said.

"I got all the help I need," he said, his voice slurred. He struggled to his feet and looked at Tanto who had pulled his legs in and actually looked apologetic.

"Damn vampire," the drunk said. "You're always in the way." He moved toward Tanto and balled up his right fist.

"That's really not accurate," I said gently.

He looked back at me quizzically, halting where he was.

"I mean really only 78.2 percent of Ventons are in the way all the time."

"What are you talking about?" he asked, squinting at me, his attention diverted from Tanto.

"I'm talking abut generalizations. Ventons aren't always in the way any more than you're always drunk and disgusting. This one Venton was in the way this one time. It's hardly enough to base a statistical analysis on." I turned to Berto and said, "Don't you just hate people who stereotype? They're all a bunch of idiots."

Berto grinned nervously.

"Disgusting?" the drunk repeated, anger finally penetrating his stupor and reaching his eyes. "You defending this runt?"

"Did I say 'disgusting?' Oh, I'm sorry. I meant to say 'nauseating.' "

He took another swing at me and I dodged it, too. "Look,"

I said. "Why don't you just go home and sleep it off? We've both said things we didn't really mean."

In answer, he swung at me again. I moved so he hit my shoulder a glancing blow. It didn't hurt, but it did give me an appreciation for the strength behind it.

"Hey," I said. "You really have a good punch there. No, I mean it."

I guess we all have to live with our guilt. His drunken, quizzical expression was actually starting to show a little pride when I hit him in the stomach, quite hard. "Did I say 'punch?' I'm sorry. I meant to say 'paunch.' "

He couldn't breathe. I helped him to a nearby table. As I leaned him onto a chair, I said, "You'd better be careful. Carrying a grudge like that, you could get a hernia."

On my way back past Berto and Tanto, both of them looking dazed, I said, "Thanks again for the conversation. See you around, Berto. I'd recommend you two get out of here before he's ready to roll again."

At the counter, I paid for the drinks and pointed back at the drunk, saying, "You really shouldn't let your customers get so drunk in here. That guy stood up and fell right over on his face. Probably damaged your floor."

The barman shook his head and started for our friend.

In the usual melodrama, when someone comes out of a bar this late at night, darkness swirls around the foggy street lights, dim alleys reek of foreboding. Outside, the hot sun over Dallad beat down unmercifully, not caring whether it was noon or midnight.

Not long afterward, I did hear mysterious footsteps behind me, though. And a voice called, "Hey, bug eye."

I looked around, but instead of Berto it was Tanto. He caught his breath from the short run. "About those artifacts," he said.

"Yes?"

"I think you should talk to a guy called Artemus. Down on East Market."

"Thanks, Tanto."

4

Undercover Operation

I.

May I Speak to You Alone?

I started looking for Artemus early the next morning. I hadn't slept particularly well; I never did on Tankur. It shouldn't have been any more difficult than adjusting to an interstellar cruise with the lights arbitrarily turned off every "night." But I always knew, as I lay in bed, that just beyond the walls of my apartment was the brightness I had always associated with day.

Partly to get out of the heat, I ate breakfast in an inexpensive diner near East Market. I thought about Rummel Hurdt's comment on my digestion, but I ate too fast anyway. I was eager to get going. This case still looked simple, and I wanted to wrap it up quickly.

"Ever hear of someone named Artemus?" I asked the cashier as I paid for my indigestion.

"No. We don't carry them. Try down the street at Osmond's."

I frowned, looked closely at the clerk and decided I had heard correctly. His expression was entirely innocent. "Thank you," I said as I double-checked my change. "I think the rain in Tripoli is tighter than a dozen hamsters."

"You're welcome," the cashier said, smiling broadly. "Have a nice day."

I should have realized that when a day starts out the way this one had it usually gets worse. My next stop was one of the small merchants near the end of East Market. The proprietor communicated clearly but knew nothing of value. I walked deeper into the market, passing closely by all the stands selling perishables because they usually had awnings that broke the heat for a moment.

As I walked, a light dust-rain began. Thermals near high noon sometimes kick dust into the upper atmosphere, and occasionally we would be treated to the fine, light dust dropping from a clear sky.

At least we have an atmosphere for dust to fall through. On some planets like Tankur, the atmosphere freezes out on the dark side. Luckily, Tankur's small size and remaining volcanic heat keep that from happening here.

The noise level and confusion grew as I made my way farther along. Most of the shops were open by now, selling everything from homemade wine to weapons. The stores along the walls were permanent establishments with locking doors. Down the center of the street were tents, moveable display tables, and people who simply unfolded a rug and placed their merchandise on it.

Youngsters of four cultures wound their way among numerous adults. Most of the kids were playing, but a few were advertising the stores their folks owned or were running errands.

One pair of young Ventons was obviously not getting along too well. A Venton crying is a pitiful sound. Their voices rise so high when they cry that even some adults sound like human babies crying. One had just hit the other hard enough to make him cry. As the one who had been hit ran, the other chased him. I stopped where I was, increasing the odds that they would pass near me. I was right. As they sped past me, I started forward again, taking a long stride.

"Oh, sorry about that," I said as the chaser spilled awkwardly on the ground. I helped him up, apologizing still more. "You're sure you're OK?" I asked with concern in my voice, gripping his arm tightly.

He tried to see which way his friend had gone, but I was

insistent enough with my apologies and concern for him that
the other was completely out of sight before we parted. He
sped away in the direction of his friend. Once he was well
away from me, he paused just long enough to make a rude
gesture at me. I shook my head and grinned and walked on.

Bertram's was only a few doors farther along. I walked in,
feeling grateful that the human proprietor had at least compro-
mised on the temperature. It was a little too cool for most
folks and a bit too warm for me.

The store was crammed about as full as it could possibly
be. Narrow aisles led between high shelves lined with more
trinkets and works of art than some museums I've been in. I
couldn't think of an art form not represented. I walked along
an aisle, pausing briefly to examine a small sand painting.

"Do you see anything you like?" asked a voice behind me.

"I always do," I said, turning.

Bertram was a white-haired, frail-looking old man. "Is
there anything in particular I could show you?"

I described the two artifacts that Kate's friend had pur-
chased here.

The smile went out of Bertram's face. "Those are already
sold."

"Yeah. I know that. I was wondering if you could tell me
where they came from."

Bertram stiffened. "I don't reveal my sources."

"I really would like to know," I said.

"I don't care. Go ahead. Beat it out of me. Or start
breaking more merchandise. I won't tell you."

Admittedly my physique makes some people think I can
get anything I want just by being physically abusive, but this
honestly seemed to be an overreaction. I said, "But you *are*
telling me someone else was here, threatening you?"

"Sure, pretend. Pretend you are not his associate." Bertram's jawline hardened. "Get out of my store."

I made no move for the door. Instead I reached for my
pocket. Bertram squinted at me as though he thought I was
going for a needler. I pulled a card from my pocket and gave it
to him. "If you change your mind, would you give me a call?"

Bertram seemed so relieved that it was a card instead of a
weapon that he glanced at it. I turned toward the door and
was almost there when he said, "Wait."

I turned around.

He was rubbing the card between his fingers. "This card. It says 'Ben Takent.' That's you?"

"No. I'm just his stunt double."

"You're kidding, right?"

"Yeah. It's a stupid little game I play. I tell people my right name and hope they'll trust me."

"Ben Takent. The guy they call 'bug eye'?"

"That's me. Is that good or bad?"

"You can prove you're Ben Takent?"

"Why? You got an inheritance for me?" I withdrew my ID card and pressed my thumb against it. It was still glowing orange as I showed it to him.

He looked at me intently for a moment before he said, "Altaherik works for me. He's a Derjon kid. You cleared his mother of a murder accusation last year."

"That's another of my stupid little games. I figure out who I'm going to need information from, and then I do them an indirect favor a year earlier. It pays off, but you have no idea of the planning it takes."

"I'll tell you some things if you'll stop with the jokes."

"Sounds fair to me. How long do I have to stop for?"

Bertram glared at me.

"I'm stopped. I'm stopped."

He waited a long moment, as though to make sure I was really going to be quiet. Finally he said, "I don't know the name of the guy who sold me those two items, but I can describe him."

I nodded.

"He's a human, maybe half a head shorter than you. Real skinny. Hardly tanned at all. Pale as a Venton. You know how rare that is here. He's younger than you, but at least twenty. He wears a ring with an 'A' on it."

"Does he come around often?" Maybe Artemus and this guy were one and the same.

"Maybe every couple of weeks."

"Would you call me if you see him again?"

Bertram nodded.

"Let me back up a minute. There was someone else in your store wanting to know about this guy?"

"Three days ago. Muscular guy, like you. That's why I

thought you were together. You know, doing the bad-guy/
good-guy routine."

"You notice anything special about him?"

"Short hair. Shorter than most. It was dark hair. Nothing
else special."

"What was he wearing?"

"T-shirt and long pants, same as you. I think his shirt was
green."

"And you never told him what you told me?"

Bertram stood a little straighter and shook his head
emphatically.

"If you see the guy who brought in the knife and the box
again, would you give him my name and tell him I'm a well-
paying collector who would be interested in more items like that?
You could tell him I promised you a ten-percent finder's fee."

"I could tell him twenty percent."

"I thought you didn't have a sense of humor."

Bertram agreed to tell him and to call me if he saw the thug
again.

Outside, my instincts told me it had to be early afternoon,
and this still seemed to be a simple case, which just goes to
show you how reliable my instincts were lately. It was barely
an hour after breakfast time. Maybe I needed a desk job near
a heat-exchanger repair place.

I walked down the street to a larger store in competition
with Bertram's. No one there remembered anyone trying to
sell them a knife or a box.

I visited over ten more stores with the same results at each.
Wouldn't you know this Artemus would turn out not to be a
comparison shopper?

II.

Do You Have a Warrant?

I was getting so bored trying to locate Artemus, I decided to
take a break and do something with more potential for surprise. I called up several recent images from my butte-top

camera and verified that Elliot Pardo was currently on duty at the dig.

Obvious clues such as the one Sam Lund had given me about Elliot having more spending money lately rarely pay off, but you can never ignore them. So I found where Elliot lived.

He rented an apartment in a building more run-down than mine. I trudged up the dirty stairs to the third floor and walked along the smelly corridor until I reached the door with the tag saying "E. Pardo." If I had a place like this, I didn't know if I'd want to use my right name.

The locks were standard, which meant that a flexible card was inadequate, but a few moments with a simple tool were enough to accomplish the task. I stepped into Elliot's apartment.

The first thing I was aware of was that Elliot's heat-exchanger worked better than the one in my office. The second was that Elliot's apartment interior was a good deal more luxurious than I would have expected.

Actually, it was a mixture of cheap and expensive. The appliances were the worst. The refrigerator looked like it would hold no more than a couple cartons of drinks and would probably not cool any more than that. Elliot's stove was a countertop burner and a toaster.

The music system and the video equipment were among the finest I'd seen. Each item was clearly protected by an integral motion-triggered warning module. Drinking glasses Elliot had casually left in the main room were laser-etched ever-crystal.

The rest of the place followed the same pattern: dumpy stuff mixed in with items far more expensive than most guards I knew could afford.

A calendar screen in the kitchen showed Elliot's work schedule. He was halfway through a string of regular shifts. Before that he had been on lates. After regulars he would be on laters.

I started looking in earnest. There was nothing under or behind his sink other than dirty slime. I sailed through a list of easy places including under the bed, beneath cushions, false bottoms in drawers, and fake outlets. Under a low shelf in the bedroom I found a gun.

This was not your everyday guard gun. Guards didn't need spreaders. This gun was so vicious that not only did the laser have enough energy to travel all the way through the victim's body, it also featured a rotating mechanism to send pulses at angles slightly away from the primary aim. Close up, the effect was like a shotgun blast.

I put the gun back where I had found it and kept looking. It took me almost an hour to make the second find.

In the narrow space over the kitchen cabinets, there was a small black box. Engraved on its cover were a large square and two smaller circles. Elliot had been a bad boy.

I put the box back where I had found it. Outside in the sun and heat, I wondered what the link between Elliot and Artemus was. And who the third guy could be.

III.

I Asked You
Never to Call Me Here

I stopped by my office to see if there were any messages. There wasn't one from the heat-exchanger people, but there was one from Morgan, whoever he was, returning my call. I called back, and this time he was out again. I left a message saying I had tried to return his call.

I had a question for Kate, but I didn't want to ask her if she was at the dig and under security scrutiny. There was a way I could find out before I called, so I did. I brought up the display from the camera on top of Vandict Butte and sent it instructions to scan through all the area with motion, holding the display for one second before moving to the next.

The displays started, moving from one picture of someone I didn't know to another. One of the images showed Dr. Fenton walking along a path. Another showed Rummel Hurdt crossing his legs. Finally Kate showed up, and I temporarily locked the camera on that location. She was using a brush to remove dirt from something I couldn't make out. I called her wristcomp number and she answered with her picture turned off.

"Hi," I said. "It's your friendly hieroglyphic reader."

"Hello, yourself." My butte camera showed Kate standing up and moving away from the other person she was with. She had her blouse pulled up partway and the ends were tied so her midriff showed. She looked good.

"I need to ask you a couple of questions after you're off duty at the site."

"Sure. I'll call you about six. That OK?" It was nice that she realized immediately that I didn't want to be monitored.

"Fine. Oh, and I really like the way you're wearing your blouse."

Kate was quick. She certainly knew her wristcomp wasn't sending a picture right now. She turned reflexively to see where the image might be originating from, and caught herself as she did it. "Thank you very much," she said. "And I'll have a couple of questions for you."

I couldn't see her face, but there was humor in her voice as she said good-bye.

As long as I was at the office, I decided to review the butte camera results so far. I had my desk computer sort all the frames acquired, first by angular position and second by time. The directory told me the camera had tracked action in about fifty areas along with sporadic motion in another twenty.

The sporadic actions had been people walking from one place to another. I reviewed them as quickly as I could, seeing nothing suspicious.

After that, I found the location where Elliot had been on duty and scanned the frames that had him in motion. There wasn't a lot to see. He liked to stay in his booth. I watched him leave the booth last night and then arrive at it this morning. He did nothing suspicious as he walked either time.

Next I looked through the archived site records of people leaving the dig through the guard shack scanners. I saw no hint of concealed artifacts in the pictures.

Feeling no further ahead, I looked through the city directory for people named Artemus. If he wore a ring with an "A" on it, maybe that actually was his name. There were twelve people with "Artemus" as a first or last name. I had the computer sort them by the distance from their addresses to Bertram's and printed the ordered list.

IV.

Are You Following Me?

Once a day the actual time agreed with the apparent time. I walked along a hot and dusty side street, assured by the knowledge that it actually was early afternoon right now. The first Artemus on the list wasn't home, so I was about to visit the second.

The second, Artemus Kalcedon, lived on the ground floor, and, unless someone was impersonating him, was a middle-aged Derjon. His forehead bumps had lost the luster of youth but hadn't yet started darkening. He must have stayed indoors a lot because his skin had faded to carmine. He clicked a greeting at me as he opened his door. I clicked back an apology. Derjon speech was hard for me, not linguistically, but physically. My tongue got tired in long conversations.

If I had talked with him much longer, I would have gotten out a couple of coins to click together. Coins weren't quite so expressive, but they did the job. Whoever said "money talks" was right.

I started for the third Artemus, hoping he would turn out to be the human I was searching for. I was getting bored until I realized I was being followed.

He was fairly good. I reversed my path, and he easily stepped into a food shop as though he had been heading there deliberately. He was good enough that for a brief time I thought maybe I was wrong, but I wasn't. Three blocks away I changed direction again and saw him in a curio shop. I wondered if maybe the first Artemus had actually been home and this guy had followed me from there.

This guy fit the description of the curious and belligerent fellow who had showed up at Bertram's: short dark hair and muscular. I took a cautious look at him, glancing his way just long enough to make sure I'd recognize him again even if he should take the drastic measure of changing his shirt, and walked on.

I resumed my walk toward the third Artemus, but, two corners later, I stopped to wait for my follower. A shaded portico provided concealment and relief from the direct sunshine.

I waited twenty minutes, and he never showed up. Maybe realizing that I spotted him twice was enough to make him more cautious. I gave him twenty more minutes and then went on my way.

The third Artemus was out, too. This was worse than being in door-to-door sales. Even on the ones I found, I wasn't getting a commission.

V.

Don't Go. It's a Trap.

Kate didn't seem terribly surprised when I told her about Elliot's misconduct. We talked about it over dinner that night.

"Elliot's been with us for more than a year," she said. "I wonder what else he's taken."

"I don't know. If he started collecting before the perimeter guard went in, he could have quite a bundle somewhere by now."

The waiter arrived with the main course. "Your chips," he said, setting them before us with a flourish.

Plants on Tankur liked the hot and dry atmosphere about as much as I did, so most of them grew down from the surface rather than up, reaching deep to get to the water table. Chips came from the thick root of a plant which, from the surface, looked more like a patch of grass than anything else, but when the root was sliced into disks and the pieces fried, they were quite good.

"So," Kate said. "What next?" She had changed from her work clothes, and, instead of her midriff showing, her shoulders were bare. She had nice shoulders, too.

"I'd like to talk to Elliot. But not in his apartment with that gun there and not in his booth where he has easy access to weapons."

"Where, then?"

"Can he be assigned temporarily tomorrow? To some duty where he doesn't need a weapon?"

"Don't like rough stuff, huh? A big guy like you?"

"I've seen enough of it."

"Like what?"

I took another bite of a chip and finished it before answering. "That company I told you about for one. They had such bad turnover, they gave out five-month pins. The place was so hectic people never left messages in IN baskets. They always left them on people's chairs because everyone was always out of the office fighting another fire."

"Why is it I don't believe you?"

"I don't know. This place was rough. It was so rough all the highway signs had laser holes through them. In town."

I was saved from having Kate tell me she didn't believe me by a call on my wristcomp. "Hello," I said. The video was off, so I left mine off, too.

"Is this the private defective?" a voice asked.

"Private *detective*," I said.

"Whatever. You want to know abut the guy you're hunting, you be at Moldern and Wetzel at midnight."

"How about if you just tell me now? I'm tired." I looked over at Kate. Her eyes were wider than I had seen them.

"Can't," the voice replied. "Be there at midnight."

"OK," I said. "How will I know you?"

"Don't worry about it. Do all you private defectives worry a lot?"

"That's detective."

"Whatever. Be there."

"OK. But give me a few extra minutes if I'm late. I don't know if I can get there that soon."

The caller terminated the call without saying anything more.

Kate reached over and touched my arm. "Don't go, Ben. That sounds like a setup if I've ever heard one. That's a terrible place to be even when there are more people around to be witnesses."

I looked at her clear gray eyes. "You're sure?"

"Absolutely."

I ate a bite of another chip. "OK. I won't go."

"Just like that? I had this vision of you refusing."

I smiled at her. "I never had any intention of going.

Maybe you watch too much melodrama. A guy could get killed going out every time some ginzo calls and says to meet him in a bad place.''

''You never—but you told him you might be a little late.'' She was beginning to grin, too. She brushed her hair behind her ears.

''If he's going to waste my time while I'm eating dinner, the least I can do is waste a little of his.''

Kate raised her glass. ''To not wasting time.''

I touched her glass with mine. I looked into her gray eyes and repeated, ''To not wasting time.''

''Where *had* you planned to be at midnight?'' she asked, her gaze level with mine.

''Well, I had considered the possibility that tonight you might get lucky.''

Kate lost some of her decorum as she laughed and choked at the same time.

VI.

My Place or Yours?

''For a strong guy, you're more tender than you look,'' Kate told me much later, in bed at her apartment. She must have liked throw pillows a lot. She had them all around the room.

''That's funny,'' I said. ''Looking at you I wouldn't have guessed you judged books by their covers.''

The corners of Kate's mouth turned up. ''You really don't like stereotyping, do you?''

''How would you like it if you thought I was here just because you're an attractive archaeologist? Don't you think you have any qualities that make you special, unique?''

''Mmmm,''she said. ''Is that why you became a detective? To cure the universe of its nearsightedness?''

''Maybe I just had latent private-eye tendencies.''

''Tell me the truth. No more evasion.''

''That's partly true. I found out I have this knack for solving puzzles. I came to Dallad to get out of a rut. When I got here, I thought about ways to make a living. You can't find many fields where you can be your own boss and open an office for less than it costs to start a one-man detective agency. I used to hate people who broke the important rules; now I specialize in them.''

She considered that for a moment. "Maybe you're specializing too much. You remember what you said about the center of the dig being special?'' Kate's bedroom was dim, lit only by a tiny strip of light at the top of her ceiling. Her eyes were focused on mine.

I nodded.

"You were right. We had considered digging there earlier, but postponed it so we could do a more thorough job on another area we had just uncovered. I convinced Dr. Fenton to go ahead and start a crew there. This—yesterday afternoon they found a cache buried two meters below the surface. It contained maybe the best finds we've made so far.''

"If my guess is right, it contained a large, inscribed cube with two circles and one triangle on each face.''

Kate's mouth opened. "That's incredible. How did you know?''

"I've done a lot of reading about Womper history, what little there is of it. I know a lot about the way they do things, and I can extrapolate to things they used to do in the past. Not only that, but I've got an incredibly good camera on top of the butte.''

"You animal! I meant to ask you if that was how you knew the way I was dressed today. I suppose you got a good view down my shirt, too.''

"I'm insulted. Besides, you hardly ever turned that direction.''

"Well, if you'd told me where the camera was—''

I grinned at her in the dim light and traced a finger down her shoulder. "Maybe we should get some sleep. I plan to have a heart-to-heart with Elliot later today. I might need my strength.''

"Maybe," Kate said softly.

5

Dead Men Tell No Tales

I.

I Didn't Think It Was Loaded

The next day was a day like any other day, at least as far as the constant heat and sunlight were concerned. Much as I hated to, I gave my wristcomp the command to allow calls through again. Someone had called me around one but hadn't left a message. That wasn't too surprising.

I sat beside Kate, who was driving, and tried to maintain a balance between resting my eyes and keeping my end of the conversation going. "Don't you get tired of this drive?" I asked as I shifted position to get more comfortable. My needler felt unfamiliar at my hip.

"No," she said with more energy than I felt at the moment. "I like it. Somehow it lets me feel that when I'm at the dig I'm isolated, far away from civilization, or at least far from modern civilization. I can imagine myself being one of the ancient archaeologists exploring pyramids on Earth. If the dig were just a kilometer from the edge of Dallad, I couldn't fool myself."

"But you know that's what's happening."

"Sure. But fantasies don't have to be perfect. They're fragile, so you do what you can to eliminate the obvious cracks in the foundation. And it isn't like I'm dependent on

59

the façade. It just makes the job a little more exciting. How can that hurt?''

"I guess I can't see anything wrong with it. Unless maybe I have to act the part of some desert camel-salesman.''

"Not required. Just finding out from Elliot what's been going on and stopping it is plenty.''

Vandict Butte rose in the shiny and wavering distance ahead. "So Sam Lund will have changed the duty roster before Elliot gets out today? Did he say what Elliot's assignment will be?''

"He wasn't sure. Sam wanted him to do a perimeter inspection so you'd have some privacy, but he hadn't had a chance to see if that would cause schedule problems.''

Soon, Kate pulled the university skimmer to a halt in front of the trailer. Just before I got out, I said, "Last night was good. Maybe we should do that again sometime.''

With a perfectly straight face, Kate said, "Yes. I'd forgotten how much I like chips.'' And then she grinned.

I had been wrong about assuming her simple corners-turned-up smile was as powerful as it got. If I had to be wrong about one thing a day, though, I wished it would be about things like that.

In the trailer, a couple of people I didn't know were eating a casual breakfast at their desks. Kate guided me along the corridor. Posted on a screen in the back room was a duty roster. Kate pointed to the line for Elliot. He was assigned to checking the perimeter.

"What actually does that mean?'' I asked. "He sees if anyone has dug a tunnel underneath the sensors?''

"That's about it. He'll also do some tests to make sure the system is functioning correctly—setting off the alarm by walking through at various points.''

"What's to stop someone from tossing out a trinket at the same time?''

"Nothing, I suppose, except trust that the security team is ethical.''

"Maybe that's how Elliot has been operating.''

"I don't know,'' she said. "It seems a little risky. Almost anyone could be watching while he tried it.''

"True. Maybe it's time I stopped speculating and went out to see him.''

Kate nodded, looking unhappy.

We walked far enough to see the dig and the surrounding perimeter poles. Almost at the far side of the dig was a lone figure near the edge.

"See you in a little," I said.

Kate opened her mouth.

I said, "Be careful, right?"

She nodded, giving me a wry grin.

I began walking around the dig, keeping several meters away from the poles. I didn't expect a lot of trouble from Elliot, but I took my needler off my belt loop and fastened it on my sleeve holder. It felt a little uncomfortable aiming up my arm, but a sharp flip of my wrist would snap it out, next to my palm.

The perimeter was almost as well traveled as the paths. A narrow, heavily footprinted track rose and fell as it crossed small mounds and depressions in the sand. Up ahead, inside the perimeter, stood a man I recognized. Sam Lund still wore his white explorer's hat.

"I'll be nearby to back you up," he said softly enough that I almost didn't hear him. I nodded slightly and walked on. I cleared my throat. Once when I looked back, Sam was making his way toward Elliot.

Naturally, Elliot was making his sweep in the same direction I was walking, so I had to go more than halfway around the perimeter. Periodically, he spoke into his wristcomp and then poked a finger or arm through the barrier. Each time he did, a loud *ping* sounded from far in the distance.

"Hi, Elliot," I said when I got close enough to talk comfortably.

"Ben, right?" Elliot looked even hotter than I felt. His shirt was open and he wore sandals. He had unattractive toes.

"Right. Mind if I ask you a few questions?"

"What kind of questions?"

"Questions like 'who's Artemus?' "

"That's not a question. That's a riddle." Elliot had stopped his series of communications to whomever he had been talking with and gave me his full attention. He scratched his neck. "What do you want?"

"I want a cooler that works. But first I'd settle for an explanation about the box in your apartment."

"I don't know what you're talking about, man. You'd better just clear out of here." Elliot's voice turned harsh. He rubbed his chin with one hand and then scratched a spot on his back. His biceps glistened with early morning sweat.

"Don't worry too much about the box, Elliot. I'm really more interested in—"

Elliot rushed me. In the distance, the perimeter alarm sounded, but I paid it no attention.

I didn't use my needler. I'd handled my share of guys like Elliot. He looked so angry that he certainly wouldn't be thinking clearly.

I was right. I easily dodged him, jabbing his kidneys fairly hard as he stumbled past. More quickly than I expected, he swung back toward me. He took a swing, and I blocked it. I punched him in the stomach, growing confident.

Only a moment later, I realized I had underestimated Elliot. Rage on his face, he moved in fast, swinging incredibly hard and fast. He hit me on the chin and again in the stomach too fast for me to defend myself. I thought about my needler and tried to spin away from him.

He knocked me over and I whirled into the dust. Before I could even start to get up, he was there kicking me in the back. Finally, I snapped my needler out from my wrist. I rolled away from his feet, partly covering my head with my left arm, and fired at his torso.

Events suddenly snapped back into real time. Elliot stood motionless for a moment, clutching his ribcage, and slowly he toppled. I was so dazed that I didn't even move away as he fell on me.

I struggled out from beneath Elliot and saw that Sam Lund was almost there.

"Roll him over so he doesn't suffocate," I said. Elliot lay facedown in the dust.

Sam kneeled beside Elliot and turned him over. It was a bit of a struggle since Elliot was a lot heavier than Sam, but he made it.

I rose to my feet shakily, deciding I hadn't suffered any permanent damage. "Shouldn't you give the medics a call?" I asked. "He's not going to feel very good when he wakes up."

Sam was feeling Elliot's wrist. He turned to me and said, "He's not going to be waking up. You killed him."

"That's impossible," I said, my mouth even more dry than normal. "I only use an anesthetic." I sat down heavily next to Elliot and felt for a pulse. His artery was still. I felt suddenly nauseated. I was lucky to be sitting down.

"I can't believe it," I said numbly. I grabbed Elliot's other arm and felt desperately for a pulse in it. Nothing. Not even aware of the pointlessness, I felt his neck. Elliot was dead.

It was a fair indication of my state of shock that as I bent Elliot's neck back and moved his arms that the distastefulness of mouth-to-mouth resuscitation didn't even occur to me then. I pounded his chest a few times, trying to remember the exact procedure, and then I began to breathe into him.

I almost hyperventilated at first, subconsciously breathing too fast. Finally I slowed down to the correct pace.

Minutes later, Elliot was clearly in no better shape than he had been. I gave up and sat there, dazed.

With one hand, Sam swept his hair back over his bald spot. "It was clearly a case of self-defense," he said.

"What?" I said.

Sam repeated what he had said.

I was aware of motion beyond him. People had stopped their activities and had come over to see what was happening.

Sam rose and turned to them. "Go on back to work. Elliot Pardo's dead, but it was his own fault."

The collective voice of the crowd murmured before the body of them began to split up and retreat. Sam and Elliot's body and I were left there in the hot sun. I wondered what Elliot had thought and felt just before he died. Had he even realized he was dying?

Sam used his wristcomp to call the police, and I just sat there, oblivious to the sun and the heat.

II.

Never Say Die

It took the police what seemed to be a long time, but they flew out to the site, so it couldn't have been more than a half-hour. I was still sitting beside Elliot's body when they walked up.

I had recovered somewhat, so I rose and introduced myself.

Elliot's lifeless body was taken away while they split Sam and me, one to a policeman. The one with me asked enough questions to get the story out. I failed to mention the box in Elliot's apartment, because it didn't really seem to matter anymore, and I would have had to tell him how I saw it. Finally he acted satisfied with what he'd heard. He'd known of cases where anesthetic darts had coupled with allergic reactions, or a high adrenaline level in combination with the allergic reaction had caused similar deaths. Not many, but enough to know that it does happen.

The two policemen compared notes, obviously looking for discrepancies between my story and Sam's. Finally they invited me to come into town with them and answer a few more questions.

In Dallad they asked me the same old things they had already asked, rephrasing after rephrasing, until I was exhausted.

When they finally released me, I walked from the police airstrip to East Market. I felt giddy, as though I were seeing through someone else's eyes. I walked from one concentration of life to the next. Whenever I looked around and saw I was in an empty space, I turned toward the largest throng I could see and walked into it. Maybe I thought Elliot's death had rubbed off on me, and I needed to cleanse myself in crowds of life.

I walked for hours. I didn't even care if my heat exchanger worked when I started back for my office.

I entered the shadowed street and walked slowly toward my door. I was almost there before I realized someone was sitting on the steps that led down to my office. Kate.

"Hi," she said, her voice husky.

"Hi," I said.

"I tried to call."

"I had my wristcomp shut off."

"Aren't you going to invite me in?" she asked after I said nothing more.

"Sure. Sure. Come on in." I stepped past her and unlocked the door, swinging it open. It was almost as hot inside as outside. If I cared about the temperature, maybe I was recovering. Kate came in behind me and I closed the door. "Are you all right?" she asked.

"Fine. Fine. And you?"

"You're not all right, are you? I'm sure you're feeling bad about Elliot's death, but is anything else wrong?"

"Anything else? I *killed* a man today. Elliot Pardo will never breathe again. He'll never complain about the cooling or look at another artifact again."

"But I still don't understand. I'm sorry he's dead, but does this always affect you this way? You're a strong man in a dangerous profession. I'd have thought you of all people would have gotten used to it."

I looked at her and said, "I don't know. Maybe I will. But I've never killed anyone before."

Kate's mouth opened in surprise. She closed it and then opened it again as though to speak, but shut it once more without saying anything. She came over and put her arms around me and hugged me. I hugged back, so hard that she had to make me loosen my grip.

Finally she said, "Let's go have dinner somewhere."

I nodded, amazed that it was already that late in the day.

III.

Thanks. I Needed That.

Kate and I talked very little during the meal, but when the waiter had cleared away the last of the dishes, she said, "How did you get into this business anyway if death bothers you so much?"

"For one thing, I didn't realize it would until now. Seeing a dead body isn't quite the same thing as being personally responsible for its condition." I took a sip of coffee. "Puzzles were what attracted me to the job. Puzzles and the sense of satisfaction of solving a problem for someone."

"You don't have the physique of someone who spends all his time solving puzzles."

I refrained from commenting on stereotyping directly. "I like the feeling of being able to take care of myself. That doesn't mean I like to beat up on people or that my brain has turned into an interstellar void."

Kate leaned back in her chair. "Is there anything I can do to help?"

"I don't know."

"Where's your sense of humor gone now? You seem to find humor in everything you see."

"Sometimes I think my sense of humor as you call it is a curse. I don't try to entertain people. I just say what occurs to me. That may or may not be funny to anyone else in the universe, so some people think I'm trying to make them laugh, and they're disappointed when I don't."

"Well, I like it," she said. "And I think you shouldn't feel so much guilt over Elliot. Guilt is like pain—they're both supposed to make you think about what you just did and to be more careful. Neither is meant to cripple. And don't give me any of that 'that's easy for you to say' junkola."

I looked into her gray eyes, and her smile took the sting away.

"Sam transferred the fee into your account," she continued. "He said that Elliot's response was a good enough admission of guilt for him—that and your finding the box. Maybe you could use the money on something to soothe your conscience."

"Maybe I could. But I'm not taking any of it until I'm finished."

"Until—what do you mean?"

"Just that. I'm not finished with this. There's a dead man I left behind today, and I'm not going to forget about him until I understand everything that's going on here."

"What's to understand? You found out Elliot's been stealing. When you confronted him, he attacked you. The case is closed. Sam's already told everyone who you are and what you were doing out there.''

"If the case is closed, what about Artemus and the guy who's been following me? And who called me the other night?''

"Who's Artemus?'' Kate asked.

"I don't have the vaguest idea. I'm really some detective, aren't I? Maybe I *am* a defective.''

"Don't say things that aren't true. But what about money? I don't think Sam wants to spend any more.''

"Ask me if I care.''

Kate leaned forward and looked at me intently. The corners of her lips turned up and she said, "Do you care?''

I had to smile. "Well, when you put it that way, maybe I do care.''

IV.

Walls Have Ears

I stopped by my office again the next morning and called the heat-exchanger repair place. "When are you going to get out here?'' I asked. "I'll call Henrod's if it isn't soon.''

"Henrod's is just one of our other shops,'' the receptionist told me. "So it wouldn't do you any good. We're trying to get to you, and we'll be there as soon as we can.''

"OK,'' I said, resigned. "It must be the summer rush season, huh?''

The receptionist looked puzzled, so I said, "Never mind. Just hurry, will you?''

Whoever this Morgan person was had called back again and left another message. I probably wouldn't have tried him this time if I hadn't wondered if it could relate to the case. He was out. I should have known. Irritated, I left a message.

I looked up Morgan in the directory. His full name was Dell Morgan, and he was listed as an independent business-man, which told me nothing.

I had the computer bring up pictures from my camera and

filtered all but the ones taken during the ten minutes before Elliot fell dead. Before I killed Elliot. There were about fifteen concentrations of activity until the fight started; then almost everyone within hearing distance was moving toward us. I sorted the pictures by their coordinates and watched each sequence by itself. Sometime the motions were jerky when there was a gap of undetected activity.

I spent most of the time looking through the two sequences that included Sam and Elliot and me. I didn't know what to look for, and I found nothing that made me sit up straight. The fight progressed the way I remembered it. Sam was there, approaching more quickly as the fight started, his back to the camera. I couldn't detect anything suspicious.

After that, I resumed my search for Artemus. The morning went as fruitlessly as before, but I knew I was doing the right thing to keep my sanity. If I just stopped and let Elliot's death eat away at me, I'd be worse off.

By noon I was sure that Artemus numbers five through nine on my list were not the person I sought. Numbers one and three were still not home. Watching for the fellow who had followed me earlier, I decided it must be number one or number three and resumed my search.

Number one was simply asking for a break-in. The lock on his door was terribly cheap. It took me under twenty seconds to get in.

The apartment was cheaper than Elliot's but without the touches of extravagance. Despite the high temperature, I looked carefully at the kitchen and bathroom first. When I finally looked in the living room, I was sure I was in the wrong place. The guy I was looking for was human, but the family pictures here were candid shots of a Derjon family.

On my way out, I loosened the doorjamb and inserted a folded piece of paper behind it before retightening it. Now maybe it would take the next person several minutes to break in.

I began the walk to Artemus three. Once, when I stopped to shake some sand out of my shoes, I thought I glimpsed the fellow who had been following me earlier. Then the heat shimmers made me decide it was only an illusion. I kept a closer watch during the rest of the trip but saw nothing more.

Artemus three lived in a top-floor apartment on a shabby

street. I knocked on the door, but there was no answer. Almost as soon as I broke in, I was sure this was the right Artemus. On one kitchen wall was a picture taken from somewhere near the dig. Vandict Butte showed in the background.

Artemus's apartment was furnished cheaply but with apparent skill in picking out the most for the money. The living room chairs looked sturdy and comfortable. The appliances in the kitchen were basic models, kept clean and in good working condition.

Actually, they weren't entirely clean. There was a little undisturbed dust on the counters, enough to indicate Artemus hadn't been there for at least a few days.

I searched the rest of the apartment, taking my time about it, looking for a clue to where Artemus might have gone. I wouldn't have been all that surprised to find his dead body concealed in the apartment, but I didn't. Nor did I find much of value. There were no names of acquaintances left out anywhere, no bills due, no club memberships. His computer was locked, and it would take far more effort than the door had taken and probably take more skill than I had in that area.

On the chance that he would be back, I pulled a tripper out of my wallet and stuck it on the top of the door frame, positioned unobtrusively so it would alert me if the door opened.

I opened the door myself and left. On my way down the stairs, I checked my wristcomp to make sure it had recorded the door opening, and it had. I set my wristcomp to sound off if it happened again.

I met no one on the stairs going down. I stepped out into the hot sun, wondering if I had just wasted another half-day. The private eye business is a lot like advertising. Only ten percent of your efforts seem to pay off, but you never know in advance which ten percent it will be. Except in my case, the ten percent might not even do that. An efficiency expert would go crazy if he had to do my job.

V.

Shut Up and Get in the Car

I went crazy doing my job. For four days there hadn't been a peep from the tripper in Artemus's apartment. I deliberately walked around town, especially East Market, to see if my follower would show himself again, but he didn't.

I probably spent more money on cold drinks than Elliot had earned in his job in a week, at least in his honest job. I went back to Bertram's to see if he could remember anything else that might help me, but he couldn't. I had looked up Artemus's last name in the Dallad city directory, and he was the only one with that surname.

I was sleeping, dreaming of Elliot falling down the side of a cliff, when my wristcomp sounded. The dual tone told me instantly it was the tripper. I got out of bed so fast my vision darkened for a moment, and then I was moving toward the door. I had been sleeping in my clothes, so except for not having shaved, I was nearly presentable. It was a couple of hours past midnight.

The bright sunshine outside stung my sleep-dilated eyes, and I had to squint to make my way forward for the first twenty meters. After that I was running. I burned my back as I got into my skimmer. I passed few people on the way. Most folks in my part of town preferred sleeping patterns that left them awake during business hours. It was hard enough to stave off the tiring effects of space-lag without deliberately desynching your body clocks.

I left the skimmer illegally parked, just close enough to a lot that I might be OK, and began running again, hoping not to hear the second alarm, the one telling me the door had been opened another time.

Breathing a little heavily, I reached the front of Artemus's apartment building without hearing the tone. I let myself relax and started up the stairs. Artemus's door was closed.

I moved quietly as I approached the door. From inside came muffled sounds of someone hurrying. Rather than knock on the door and alert Artemus, if that was who was here, I waited next to the door, to the far side of the stairway.

I had guessed right. The wait wasn't long. After just a few more minutes, the door opened quickly and silently. As he turned toward the stairway and started to pull the door closed, I put an arm around him and pushed him into the apartment. He yelped, obviously severely startled, but still worried about making noise.

It was Artemus. The pale, heavily breathing young man standing before me matched the description Bertram had provided. "What do you want?" he said, the bravado almost covering up the fear in his voice. "And who are you?"

"I'm a private investigator, and I want to talk to you. You know you're really a hard guy to get hold of? You really should let your secretary know where to find you."

"I've got nothing to talk to you about. Get out of my apartment." His eyes showed fright.

I took a guess. "Listen to me. The guy who's been following you, asking about you, the strong guy who roughed up Bertram—that's not me. I don't know who he is, but he's not me. I'm just a simple, *honest* private detective, and you're involved in something you and I need to talk about. This may even help you."

I had guessed right, or at least I was close enough to what was going on that Artemus lost some of his bluster.

"How do I know you're what you say you are?" he asked.

"You don't, really. But if I were that other guy, I wouldn't be civil right now. And you might even be dead."

"I've got to get out of here."

"Fine. Let's go together. You can tell me all about it when we get someplace safer."

Artemus hesitated. "OK. Let's go."

I didn't waste time. I opened the door quickly, prepared to close it again even more quickly, but there was no one in the hall. I led the way to the stairs and Artemus closed the door behind us, making no more sound than wind blowing over a smooth stone.

The street was empty. There wasn't even an insomniac out in the stifling brightness.

As we hurried away, I could see at least a couple of reasons why Artemus might be worried about this other guy.

Artemus was spindly thin, his muscles hardly more developed than those of a year-long bed-ridden patient. A strong punch would probably break a bone. I was amazed that his pale skin had not taken a tan, here of all places.

Then again he might not be so bad off. We ran the next couple of blocks toward my skimmer, and when we arrived he wasn't breathing heavily at all.

We drove five kilometers before either of us said a word. Finally, I said, "Tell me what's happened so far."

"You tell me," he said firmly. He looked just old enough to be finished with school and on his first job.

I told him what had happened so far, about Kate hiring me, about the box in Elliot's apartment, and Elliot's death. "I have this feeling you're going to wind up like Elliot if you don't let me in on what's going on," I said. "That's not a threat. It's just the way things may be."

I turned onto the main highway through town, deserted except for no more than three other skimmers. With no good reason, I had chosen the direction toward the dig.

"OK," he said finally. "It started about two weeks ago. I was out hiking."

"Near the dig? Near Vandict Butte?"

"Yes. The land around here is just too boring. So I went out there to get some variation. I thought maybe I could climb the butte, but it's too steep. I didn't want to interfere with what they were doing at the university setup, so I stayed clear. I could see them in the distance sometimes, but that was all."

Artemus swallowed hard. "Anyway, that's where I was when I found it."

"It?"

"A cache of artifacts."

It Seemed Like a Good Idea
At the Time

I.

Ashes to Ashes, Dust to Dust

I kept the skimmer pointed toward the dig. There was no one in sight behind us. "Tell me about it," I urged Artemus.

"Why are you driving this direction?" he asked.

"Depending on your description, I think we might want to take a look at it. If it sounds like a waste of time, we won't bother."

"OK," he said finally, leaning back in his seat for the first time, as though he felt relieved. "I was near the base of Vandict Butte, considering whether to try to climb it or not, when I noticed a pile of rocks that looked a little unusual, you know, like someone had stacked them. And the ground near the rocks was flattened, as though someone had walked near there several times. So I rolled away a couple of the rocks, and I found the hoard."

"And you decided to take some of it."

"Yes. Sure, maybe it wasn't right. But it didn't seem to me that whoever had left them there was honest. Who would hide a pile of artifacts in a place like that? If the university people had been there, they would have just taken them along. And I didn't take them so much as I relocated them."

"So there's more besides what you sold?" I started keeping a closer watch for anyone on the road behind us. Still no one.

"Yes. I sold only two pieces, two of the smallest. There's probably fifty more pieces still there."

"But not where you found them."

"Right."

"So that's why this guy has been after you. How did you know about him?"

"A friend at a store on East Market hears all the gossip. He told me. He also told me this guy isn't anyone to mess around with."

"What did you plan to do?"

"Grab the few things I wanted to keep and get off this planet," Artemus said. "I'm too young to die."

"Aren't we all?"

"Don't you think it might be dangerous to go out there? He might be out there, looking."

"I doubt it, after two weeks. He wouldn't know you left them out there. He's probably been concentrating on you. There wasn't any sign of him back there, so he might even think you're already gone." I hadn't brought my needler, but we could always call for help.

"I wish I were. I wish I'd never found that stuff."

"I'm glad you did. With this guy Elliot dead, I was having trouble figuring out how the thefts had been engineered and who else was involved. It sounds like the guy on your trail might be Elliot's partner. And right now, any friend of Elliot's is a friend of mine."

It was a couple of hours before breakfast as we sped toward the land of midafternoon. "How can you stand to hike in a place this hot?" I asked.

"Unusual metabolism, I guess. It probably goes with my skin. I never do get a tan, and the temperature feels good to me."

Artemus was silent as we traveled another kilometer or two, and then he said, "You know, there's something that doesn't fit. I'm not sure if this guy was in on any thefts or not."

"Why do you say that?"

"Because while I was hiking, I found several places where

someone had been digging. The piles of dirt had completely dried out, so it couldn't have been in the last day or so, but it had to be in the last few months. Why would they dig if they were stealing?''

Why indeed? I didn't have an answer.

After several more kilometers of sandy ground had flashed past us, Artemus pointed toward a dirt road on the left. We were close enough to the dig to see Vandict Butte clearly. I pulled my skimmer onto the bumpy trail, straining to see if there seemed to be recent tracks. It was hard to say. I could have done a better job if I got out to look, but I didn't want to spend the time, and I wasn't sure what I would do differently anyway.

The road grew rougher, and I had to slow down. Finally it dwindled down to nothing at the foot of a bluff. We got out of the skimmer, and Artemus gestured in the direction of the butte. "We have to go on foot from here," he said.

"Right. But let's hurry."

We kicked up dust as we made it to the top of the bluff. Beyond it, the land flattened out again, cut diagonally by a narrow arroyo that probably hadn't carried water more than a few thousand times since my ancestors first made fire.

Not far from the other side of the bluff, we had to leap over the arroyo. Fortunately, there was a place where it narrowed enough to jump without too much fear of falling down the steep sides. It was only about two meters deep at that point, but it looked as though if a person fell in, it would be hard to get out.

We traveled fast. Artemus was in excellent shape despite his apparent frailty. My mouth was dry and dusty by the time Vandict Butte looked to be as near to us as it was to the dig. The dig was about even with the right side of the butte, and we were nearly even with the left side. Tenacious, brown-stemmed plants clung to the hard-packed ground, no doubt getting far more sunlight than they needed.

"There's the first place I saw where someone had been digging." Artemus pointed ahead of us on the path where in a gentle depression there were five mounds of dirt obviously removed from the nearby hole.

Artemus was certainly right. The surface of the piles held the fine texture of dirt recently exposed to the surface. My foot easily made a print on it. The hole was about knee deep, long enough for a coffin. I stepped into it. At one end of the hole, there was exposed a short section of wall that looked very much like the ones I had seen at the university dig.

The holes had to be new, though, or else they would have shown up on the orbital views the university took before starting the dig.

"What do you think this means?" Artemus asked. "Does that ancient city take up a lot more space than the university people think it does?"

"That's certainly possible. If I weren't such a cautious guy, I might even say 'likely.' " I stepped out of the hole. "Where was the cache you found?"

"We've got a ways to go." Artemus started walking toward the butte. On the way we passed three more holes similar to the first.

Finally we reached the base of the butte. Up close, the rise from the plain to the steep sides seemed more gentle than it had looked from on top, but it obviously would require serious climbing gear to go more than twenty meters up.

"There," Artemus said, and I saw the rocks.

It was as he'd described it, except he hadn't searched as thoroughly as those of us in the business do. Nearby we found some prospecting equipment, cheap versions of the scanners the university used. One of them should provide at least a crude image of the top twenty centimeters of ground. The tool was well worn, but it wasn't decades old. Somebody had left it here recently.

"And where did you move the stuff to?" I asked.

Artemus pointed. "You see the large rock in the distance?"

"That far?"

"No. I used it as a heading. Come on."

As we walked, I occasionally looked back to see how visible our footprints were, feeling relieved that they hardly showed. Artemus caught me looking once and said, "It gets more rocky over this way. That's why I chose it."

The ground was also more irregular here, leading us up and over numerous rises followed by depressions just deep enough to make us pay attention to our bearings before losing sight of the distant boulder.

"How many trips did it take you?" I asked.

"Four. Nothing there was all that heavy."

"Weren't you worried about being found?"

"Not at the time. The stuff could have been there long enough that someone wouldn't be back for quite a while."

It didn't take much longer to reach the place where Artemus had stored the items he had taken from the cache. His hiding spot was simple, but, without knowing which rock to look behind, it could take a long time to find. And the original owner might easily believe the artifacts were no longer in the area.

Nestled between two large rocks were many more vases and cups, two ornamental boxes, and a knife. The blade of the knife was almost sharp enough to shave with. "Thanks, Artemus," I said. "If these turn out to be stolen, the university should offer you a finder's fee. And if they're not, you should get a reward anyway."

"I don't want a reward. I just want to get out of here."

"That's probably one of your best ideas lately. Give me just a minute." I shoved everything except the knife back into the hiding place. Sitting on top of one of the rocks, I took a three-way sighting on the sun, the butte top, and the large rock we had been aiming for. With the images stored in my wristcomp, I could get back here with no problem.

As we started back toward the skimmer, I pondered my selection of the knife. Whoever had hidden these items in the first place could come back out here periodically or have the place under surveillance. I almost wished I had my needler, but I still vividly remembered what had happened the last time I took it with me. Maybe I had taken the knife in response to an unconscious need for protection, although what good a knife would be against a needler was beyond me.

"Do you have any idea who the guy following you is?" I asked as we trudged through the hot, dusty sunshine.

"One of my friends thought his name was Gatlon or something. I was more interested in staying away from him than getting to know him."

"Getting to know your enemy lets you know where he might be and where he might not be."

I wasn't as good as I could be on the subject of knowing where he might not be. As we reached the arroyo and prepared to jump it again, a voice came from ahead of us and a head showed over the top of the bluff.

"Stop right there," he said. He was the guy who had followed me earlier. His voice was familiar from a late-night wristcomp call.

"Hello, Gatlon," I said, taking a small gamble.

"How did you—" He stopped before he got into even more trouble, but it was enough.

"How did I know it was you? You were easy. Even my stupid partner was able to figure it out." I had to keep him off balance, thinking he was up against more than he was, because as well as his head showing, there was a needler.

"You don't even have a partner." Good news and bad news. Gatlon was smart enough to have checked that out, but dumb enough to talk when he should have been devoting all his attention to us. I pushed Artemus over the lip of the arroyo and jumped into it beside him. I heard a faint *whoosh* of needles passing, but felt none hit.

The bad part was landing on the uneven arroyo floor below. I hit hard enough to compress carbon into diamonds.

I lifted Artemus to his feet and said, "You OK?"

He nodded.

"Good. Run that way quietly for the first hundred meters and then give it all you've got. Call the police."

Artemus nodded again and ran away from me. I turned and ran the opposite direction down the narrow arroyo, making noise as I went. The knife was in my hand, but it would be suicide to let Gatlon get near enough for me to try to use it.

At one point it wasn't hard to make noise. I slipped on loose pebbles and nearly fell. As I ran, I had to twist and turn a lot. After my near fall, I tried to stay as quiet as I could. I was already beginning to wonder if I had made the right move, but, if we had just waited there for Gatlon, the situation would have been worse.

I ran. The arroyo's sides remained steep, overhanging slightly in places. I hoped soon I'd reach a collapsed side and I could get out. If I could maintain a good distance from Gatlon, I'd be relatively safe on the surface. But right now, he could surely run faster on the ground above than I could with all the twists and turns in this narrow arroyo.

In fact, he could even be ahead of me. I might have been

better off if I stopped and began running back the way I had come. I stopped and listened. There came the vibrations from Gatlon's feet as they pounded the surface, but I couldn't tell whether he was ahead or behind. And if he came across me, there would be no contest.

I sat there an instant longer, waiting under a slight over-hang, wondering which way to run, when I suddenly realized how stupid I was being. There *was* a way I could see where Gatlon was.

My camera on top of the butte. If I were any dumber, I'd have to pay a competent private eye to fasten my shoes.

With my wristcomp, I took the camera out of its current mode and swept it to the right of the dig. When my screen showed a wide view that certainly must have contained us, I stopped and put the camera back in motion-sensing mode.

The sounds of Gatlon's footsteps intruded on me, but I still couldn't tell whether he was ahead of me or behind me. I pushed myself hard against the arroyo wall, hoping the con-cealment was adequate. I held my wristcomp near my face.

Only seconds later, Gatlon's image came up on the screen. He was partly crouched, needler in hand, near the edge of the arroyo. I couldn't tell yet where I was in the picture, but gave the command for the camera to lock onto Gatlon.

Where I had stopped, the arroyo was not straight. Here it curved gently away from me in both directions, so my hiding place should look like the turning point in a curve from on top. I looked in the camera image for a similar feature. The camera had zoomed too close to Gatlon, so I widened its field of view until the lip of the arroyo showed. Heat waves shook Gatlon's image.

Trying to make sure the optics didn't fool me into moving in the wrong direction, I decided that Gatlon had gone farther than I had. He was moving quietly now, his posture good for exploring dark alleys.

I started moving also, slowly and quietly. Gatlon was far enough from the lip that he wouldn't be able to see me. If only I could get to the next bend in the arroyo before he got close enough. Maybe he thought I was armed but had re-frained from starting the shooting because I was so exposed.

I reached the bend without feeling needles ripping into my

back. I kept running, trying to stay quiet at the expense of my top speed. I had to get out of the arroyo.

He must have heard me. One time I looked at my wristcomp, he was still carefully scouting; the next time he was running back toward the left in the camera—toward me.

I reviewed the layout of the land we had traveled over. I hadn't seen anyplace where it would be easy to get out of the arroyo. Artemus must have called the police by now, but the best they could do, unless I found a fast solution, would be to arrest Gatlon after he killed me. They're never around when you need them.

I was almost back to the place where I had jumped into the arroyo when I thought of a possibility. The arroyo was wide for most of its length, except the narrow section where we had jumped over it.

I stopped when I got back to the narrow section and hugged the wall on Gatlon's side. The arroyo was shallower here, so I could jump high enough to get my hands over the top, but the sides were too crumbly to let me get a grip and pull myself up. There might be another chance, though.

I picked up a rock near my feet. For the next several seconds I watched Gatlon on my wristcomp. When he turned his head away from the arroyo for a moment, I threw the rock.

The rock sailed out of the arroyo and landed on the ground well away from the lip. Gatlon's head jerked around, looking for the source of the sound.

Good. He obviously decided it had come from the opposite side, because he was now running for the narrow crossing point. If he jumped over, it wouldn't take him long to find out I wasn't over there, but I had other plans.

Here he came. He *was* going to leap across the arroyo, right over me.

As he jumped, so did I.

I flailed my arms for an instant as I realized I had jumped a fraction of a second too late. And then my hand clenched his ankle.

He was moving so fast his ankle almost slipped from my grip, but I held on as tightly as I could.

It worked. The unexpected weight of my body pulling him down made him miss his landing. He missed it by a lot.

Instead of his foot reaching the lip on the far side, I dragged him down far enough that his belly hit the edge. Hard.

His short surprised curse turned to a sharp cry even before he thudded against the dirt wall, and his breath left him. I released my grip and scrambled out of the way so he wouldn't fall on me. I almost made it. His other leg hit me a glancing blow as he fell backward to the bottom of the arroyo, but it was nothing to the pain he must be feeling.

I didn't give him any time to recover. As soon as he hit the ground, I grabbed his needler and put my foot against his neck. "Were you working with Elliot Pardo?" I asked.

He moaned briefly as though in pain and moved his lips soundlessly. I was too smart for him, though. I didn't kneel beside him to listen and thereby give him another opportunity.

Just seconds later, he shuddered briefly, still without speaking, and became still. Even the facial wrinkles brought on by pain faded away. I tried an experimental kick on one of his legs. No response.

Very carefully, I took hold of one wrist, feeling for his pulse.

"Damn it! Damn it! Damn it!" I hadn't realized I could yell so loud. Utterly angry with myself, I pulled the trigger on Gatlon's needler and held it down as a steady stream of needles knifed their way up the arroyo and into a dirt wall. They cut out a nice little hollow.

I couldn't believe it. After a long moment of balling and unballing my fists, wanting desperately to hit something or someone, I kneeled beside Gatlon and rolled him over. It took only a brief inspection to see what had caused his death; the back of his skull had hit a rock quite hard.

Blood had drained into the absorbent ground, leaving hardly a puddle. Ashes to ashes, dust to dust. And a good deal speedier than usual. Damn it all!

II.

And Then It Hit Me

Artemus had gone back to the bluff to wait for the police while I stayed with the body.

The policeman who arrived with him was a Venton. "Another day, another body, Mr. Takent?" was the first thing he said to me.

"This was self-defense."

He looked down at me, the sun just behind his head making it nearly impossible to see his pale features. "I've already heard that. I've been talking to your friend here. Did the victim ever actually fire at you?"

"Yes. And maybe you could pick a better label than 'victim.' The guy was trying to—"

"I see," he said.

My humor improved a tiny fraction as he spent the next minute trying to see how he could get down here to see the body. Finally, he seated himself on the edge of the arroyo and jumped.

After a brief examination of Gatlon's body, the policeman said, "I do like variety. The last one was shot with a needler, right?"

"Lieutenant—"

"Inspector."

"Inspector, I don't make a hobby out of this. The guy was after us with a needler. I did the only thing I could to stay alive. I didn't think it would kill him. I didn't *want* to kill him. I wanted to ask him some questions."

"What kind of questions?" the inspector asked. At the same time, two more shadows fell on the arroyo wall. Two more policemen.

"Come with me, and I'll talk about it, Sergeant," I said.

"Inspector," he said again.

The inspector's associates had brought a strap, so they helped us out of the arroyo, and Artemus and I took the inspector back to the cache Artemus had hidden. The inspector limped as he walked, but I didn't ask him about it. I'd had enough running and walking in the heat today and was in a quiet mood.

One of the inspector's helpers met us. Despite my desire to get out of there, the four of us had a long, hot talk. The inspector was plainly as unhappy as I was with it all, and he insisted on my coming into town for a visit at his place.

I let Artemus take my skimmer after he promised to stay available and tell Kate what had happened.

"Thanks for what you did," he said, offering his hand. "At least it's all over."

I shook his hand and said, "I'm not entirely sure. It may be just beginning."

III.

Where Does It Hurt?

When they finally let me out, I tried drinking this time. It didn't have any longer-lasting results than my efforts to cleanse myself after Elliot's death. Unless you count the hangover.

But who's counting? Certainly not me. Two deaths—two killings. Two friendly discussions with the police. And one beautiful lady.

She was waiting for me when I went back to my office.

"Hello, Kate," I said.

"I came over in case you needed someone to lean on. If you don't want me here, just say so." She sat on the steps in the shade.

"Me lean on anyone? A big, strong guy like me? A big, strong, intelligent guy like me? No way. Maybe we could lean on each other."

"Maybe we could."

"And maybe I've got more investigation results to give you."

"Like what?"

"Not yet. It's just a theory. Can we go out to the dig? Even if the case is closed?"

"What a silly question. You're a hero out there. We

wouldn't have known about the second site without you. Or have gotten those artifacts Gatlon dug up. But is tomorrow morning soon enough? We might be too busy today."

I sat down beside Kate on the steps and put my arm around her waist. My doorway needed cleaning out again, but I didn't worry about it then. I even managed to grin. "Busy doing what?"

IV.

The Plot Thickens

Maybe it isn't *always* necessary to keep the body's clocks perfectly in step with night and day. A night with Kate had made me feel more human. There had even been an hour or two when I hadn't thought about Elliot dying and Gatlon dying. Justifiable homicide, the inspector had decided about Gatlon. I thought about the word "justifiable" as Kate drove us out to the dig the next morning. I'd have to come to terms with that word, or I might have to find another occupation.

"Homicide" isn't a pretty word either.

The chart room in the trailer had received several updates since I had been there last. Next to the first dig, a second dig showed a roughly circular outline.

"That's where Gatlon had been digging," Kate said, pointing at three separate bright red blips surrounded by numerous blue markers. "The blue signifies preliminary indications of items buried near the surface. And we have another puzzle developing. The only skeletons we've found so far are adults. Not one child."

The center of the second site was roughly even with the left side of Vandict Butte. I was already fairly certain my suspicions must be correct, but I asked Kate to let me get one of the artifacts from the vault.

She was growing impatient with me by the time we got back to the chart room.

I examined the box with its markings and looked back at the hologram. I was sure I was right.

"So. Are you going to tell me now what's going on in that cranium of yours?" Kate said.

"Promise you won't laugh?"

"Is it going to be funny?"

"Not in the least."

"Then I won't laugh."

I hefted the box in my hand. "You see the pattern on the side of this box? It shows up everywhere out here."

"This?" she said. "The triangle inside a large square with the two small circles outside?"

"Yes."

"Yes, I see it. What's the point?"

"Looking around this room, does it make you think of anything?"

Kate scanned the hologram. "Nope."

"Shrink the display."

She gave me a puzzled look and complied.

"Stop," I said when the display had diminished in size to the point that the trailer was a speck. I walked toward the outline of the first dig and I held the box near the image of the plain. I turned the box so the two circles were in front of the large square. "Now what do you see?"

Kate's eyes narrowed. "I see two circles and a square and a triangle."

"And what do you see on the ground?"

"Two circles and a square." She came near me and pointed at the two round dig sites and the squarish butte thrusting up from the plain. "What exactly are you saying?"

"I'm saying that you've discovered two medium-sized archaeological sites. But there's a site buried under Vandict Butte that will make them look as tiny as a couple of graves."

7

And Then It Happened

I.

Let Me Get This Straight

"I'm glad to see you're not laughing," I said. "But maybe you could look a bit less disbelieving."

Kate looked at me in silence a moment longer. "Let me make sure I understand what you're saying." She moved nearer the butte in the hologram and pointed at it. "You're saying that because Vandict Butte is roughly square, and because the two sites are roughly circular, that means there's an enormous ancient city or something tunneled into the butte?"

"Yes, I'd say that's about it. Of course there's more to it. More explanations. But that's the right conclusion."

"You wouldn't mind if I—if I called Dr. Fenton in, would you?" She still looked as though she didn't believe a word of it.

"How quickly they turn," I said under my breath. Kate was just starting to speak when I said, "That would be Dr. Fenton the archaeologist or Dr. Fenton the psychiatrist?"

"The archaeologist." She called him on her wristcomp without waiting on my response.

As it happened, he was close by. He joined us in the chart room. Kate had evidently used the brief wait to think better of her disbelief, because she gave Fenton a factual recap of my statement without using prejudicial language. It didn't help much.

"My boy," Fenton said, giving me an immediate summary of his appreciation for my theory, "over the years, there have been many instances of lay people making guesses about what would be found at archaeological sites. I think it comes from the fact that, to an outsider, our profession looks quite easy. In fact, it's not.

"We have to be specialists, and generalists at the same time. Archaeology encompasses history, geology, meteorology, sociology, evolution, biology, zoology, botany, physics, chemistry, anthropology, paleontology, linguistics, and another dozen fields you probably know even less about. I appreciate your intentions, but we can't simply start excavating on evidence such as this."

"Would you like to hear the rest of my rationale?" I asked when he finally finished. "I may not have a degree, but have I been wrong yet?" I'd been wrong at least enough times to have long ago lost count, but I'd been lucky lately, and I pushed it.

Dr. Fenton and Kate stared at me a moment until Kate said, "Go ahead. There's nothing to lose."

I looked at Fenton long enough for him to nod, and I began. "You probably know the Womper myth involving a Garden-of-Eden-variety story about the first Wompers. In their case, the story involves being cast out of darkness into the blinding light. Maybe long ago the Wompers were cave dwellers or tunnelers. Outcasts might have had to leave the comfort of the cave and make their own way on the desert surface. They care so little for legends and history, I think it's interesting that this particular legend has survived."

"But we don't even know for certain this is the world Wompers originated on," Kate said.

"No matter. Here's a better question for you. Do either of you know the Womper symbol for birth or origination?"

Kate and Fenton looked at each other. Fenton said, "Yes, of course. It's a spiral."

"Right. And I've seen that spiral inside a triangle on several pieces here. Triangles never show up in Womper art elsewhere. I think that means those pieces aren't art. They're messages.''

"Messages?"

"Yes. The spiral inside the triangle says they came from the place marked that way. And you just saw the map with two circular sites next to a large square butte—a butte that has the triangle inside it to show that's where they originated.''

"But I'm still convinced you're making quite a leap to assume that means Womper life originated in the butte. As I said earlier—''

"Dr. Fenton,'' I interrupted. "The three of us here are all in the same business. Hermeneutics.''

Fenton raised his eyebrows.

"Yeah,'' I said. "I know a few big words even though I don't have a degree. Or at least an archaeology degree. We three are all students of hermeneutics. We all try our hands at the art of not being fooled. I try to see the truth amid the lies. You do the same. You obviously can't afford to believe in hoaxes. You could waste years by following a bad assumption or letting some cheat show you a few bones he claims he found on his property. We all try to sift the truth from the evidence.''

The frown on Fenton's face softened, and he said, "I really do appreciate all the thought you've given this. If we get a chance to check on this theory of yours, we certainly will.''

"Hermeneutics, Doctor. That's your archaeologist-explaining-to-the-head-office-empty-brains tone of voice. But it's your loss.'' I took one last glance at the hologram of the butte, placed the box in Kate's hands, and started for the door.

"Ben—'' Kate started.

"It's OK,'' I said. "I've always been able to lead a horse's ass to water. What I have trouble with is the part that comes afterward.''

"Ben—'' Kate tried again. "You're acting unreasonably.''

I looked at her face in the darkened chart room. "You know, I guess I am. Sorry, Kate. Sorry, Dr. Fenton. I'll be OK.''

"Ben,'' Fenton said. "You've given us a lot of help. We *will* make some checks.''

I felt a little better, but I was still irritated when I left. I wasn't terribly graceful about being wrong, but what really bothered me, anytime, was someone being condescending to me.

"Does it get worse from here? Are you going to tell me Fenton is going to charge me for the equipment rental?"

"You really don't like to be wrong, do you?"

"Everyone is wrong some of the time. You can be right with some of the people most of the time and be right with most of the people some of the time, but—"

"Just give me a straight answer, will you?" Kate grinned and gave me the feeling she could see through me even over the comlink.

"OK. I don't like being wrong. I get a sense of self-worth out of being right, a kind of miniature feeling of accomplishment. Is that so bad? I probably have worse faults."

"No, it's not so bad," Kate said soberly. "Especially in this case. I probably have my little faults, too." She grinned again. "Because I just lied to you."

I leaned forward.

She said, "Dr. Fenton *did* rent that equipment and make the search. But Vandict Butte isn't just rock and dirt. There's something inside. Something really big."

III.

Let's Get to
The Bottom of This

I met Kate in the chart room at the site. Dr. Fenton and Sam Lund were there with her. On my way in, everyone I'd seen had looked agitated, excited.

Even Dr. Fenton had shed some of his reserve. "OK, you can say it," he said when I first saw him.

"Say what?" I asked.

"I told you so."

"I may like to be right, but I try not to be too obnoxious about it."

Kate's face virtually glowed. She grabbed my arm and then practically shouldered Fenton and Sam Lund out of the way so I could see the rest of the hologram. "Look at that!" she said.

The image of Vandict Butte dominated the far side of the room, but the hologram had changed since the last time I had looked at it. A blue box lay outlined underneath the surface. The box was square on top. Its height was about half its width and length, as though someone had cut a cube in two and dropped one half into the core of the butte. It nearly filled the entire volume of the butte and extended a small depth below the desert surface.

"I'm not sure I understand," I said. "Is the blue surface as far as you've probed? I expected to see maybe a honeycomb of tunnels or the openings of tunnels, depending on how deep you could scan."

"Forget tunnels. This is something a lot more exciting. That's a building"

I looked at her with what was probably a stupid expression on my face.

Her voice rising, she said, "The surface there is a real surface, not some display construct. There is a fabricated *something* under the butte, and it's that large."

"And it's been sitting under your noses all this time?" I said. "Something that large should have shown up on someone's sensors before."

"Not very likely," said Dr. Fenton from behind me. "The outline you see had to be built from scans in five segments of the spectrum from three different measurement systems. Whoever left it there must have possessed the technology to make materials very difficult to detect."

He spoke a command to the hologram controller, and the rectangular solid lost its smooth sides and precise definition. Now it looked like an irregular second layer of rock underneath the real rock. "This is what it looks like when you use only one measurement type. A geologist looking closely at it can see features that don't correlate to the way buttes come into being, but no one had a good reason to look this carefully until now."

He gave it a second command and the blue solid reshaped itself into the regular structure. Sam Lund was still with us in the room, but he hadn't volunteered any information.

"But it's enormous," I said finally.

"Exactly," Kate said. "There are teams at over twenty

universities making preparations to come here, once we dig in and verify that the structure contains artifacts.''

"Where would you start on something this large?"

In reply, Kate expanded the hologram until we were looking at the side facing the original digs. With the increased scale, I could see an irregularity near ground level, centered between two walls. It looked like a small bump, poking out from the surface. "We'll try there first. It may be a door. If that doesn't work, we'll probably start digging on top of the butte."

"Incredible," I said softly, thinking of how old the structure must be.

Dr. Fenton spoke up again. "We'd like you to be there with us when we go through the door. After all, you're responsible for finding it. And you've been far better than a grumpy old archaeologist guessed you might be at solving puzzles. When Kate said your cover here would be as a problem-solver, I thought it might lack credibility. I don't like to be wrong, either, but I guess it happens to all of us."

"Do you have any idea about how long ago this was built?" I asked.

"It's hard to be precise with a time span as long as this," Fenton said, "but our first guess is on the order of ten thousand years. We'll know more after we get samples from inside the wall."

"But that age is consistent with the two outside settlements?"

"Yes."

I turned to Sam Lund who had been quiet the whole time I had been there. "Does this mean a lot larger security team?"

He turned toward me with a jerky motion, as though he had been thinking of other things and abruptly realized someone was paying attention to him. "Not necessarily. If we dig through at one point, there isn't much of a perimeter to protect. If the place is in fact filled with artifacts, then we'll have to work out a way of handling the volume of material. But things will probably go slowly at first. The only hiring we might do until then is to handle turnover." He looked at me pointedly.

I cleared my throat.

Turnover. Justifiable. Homicide. I didn't like the way Sam Lund was looking at me. Hurriedly, I asked Dr. Fenton and

Kate, "How soon do you think you'll be ready to go through the wall?"

Kate answered that one. "Three days."

IV.

Don't Hold Your Breath

On the sixth day, I was waiting as they dug the tunnel deeper. It probably wouldn't have taken so long if it hadn't been for the jurisdictional disputes among the fourteen or so unions. I had temporarily abandoned my investigation of Harry Gatlon's background; the happenings here at the dig were occupying too much of my thought, and the information search had seemed futile anyway.

I sat in the shade of the tunnel mouth, waiting for word from farther in that they had reached the goal. The tunnel itself was circular. Far inside the butte, an enormous traveling tunnel-borer swept debris toward the outside along a big conveyer belt as the borer moved slowly forward. Dr. Fenton evidently had a few friends in the mining business who owed him favors.

A large round hose fed fresh air into the deepest part of the tunnel so the stale air slowly traveled out past me as I sat. A smaller set of hoses carried the tunnel sealer compounds to the borer so it could cast an interior pipe which protected against a tunnel cave-in.

Finally, one of the workers told me the cutting crew had decided they were close enough to proceed more carefully. I left the tunnel for a while, and workers rode the borer all the way out so the crew doing the detail work could start.

Several more hours passed.

"The crew should be getting close now," Kate said from behind me. I hadn't heard her come up. "You want to go in with me?" Her clothes today appeared to be made of slightly heavier fabric than her usual attire.

I looked into the dimly lit tunnel and said, "Why not?"

The air seemed to grow slightly cooler as we walked. "Are you excited?" I asked her.

"Of course. This may turn out to be the high point of my career." She tucked her hair behind her ears.

"So it might be all downhill from here? Never again will you have the opportunity you do now?"

"Not everyone can time it so the best moment in a career comes thirty days before retirement. It can be nice to sit back once in a while and think about your accomplishments. If your big moment came just before you died, you'd never get to cherish the feeling."

I thought about it in silence as we walked several more meters. "Maybe I'd think differently about it if it weren't true that in my line of work the closer you come to that ultimate case, the closer you come to your ultimate reward in the sky."

Kate considered that. "I feel sorry for you if you don't get any enjoyment when you think back over your accomplishments. Maybe that's partly why I picked archaeology; I don't just live for the present and the future. Maybe you're really a Derjon who got mixed up at the hospital when your parents picked you up."

"Don't you think my parents would have noticed? And besides, I *do* get a sense of pride when I think back to my best moments. But why do you think humans are the race that spends the most time thinking about the past?"

"Maybe it's our competitiveness. We want to know what people before us did so we can make sure we do better."

"That sounds more like common sense than competition," I said. "Or maybe a racial survival trait."

"Sounds reasonable, but why are we alone? Why don't the other races we know have the same survival trait?" We had moved far enough into the tunnel that the portal was only a small circle of light far behind us.

"Maybe they do, but they have other stronger survival traits. Take Wompers. They are incredibly strong compared to us. They're peaceful to the point of apathy. I've never known one to die of anything but simple old age. Maybe they don't need that kind of survival trait."

"Perhaps," Kate said, kicking a solitary rock farther into the tunnel.

Finally the string of lights ahead showed a concentration. We were approaching the end of the tunnel. We walked the rest of the way maintaining our silence. I wondered what lay behind the wall, and Kate must have been curious about the same thing.

The lighting was nearly as good as daylight. At the end of the tunnel was a circular surface that was obviously not rock or dirt. It looked as though the digging team had tunneled up to the wall of a building. Except most buildings I had seen didn't have doors this size.

The exposed surface had to be a door. The door was circular, occupying about eighty percent of the cleared area. It bulged slightly out from the surface. What must be hinges bordered the left side. The surface betrayed no sign of age. It was a flat black with no sign of a handle.

The lighting on the door changed as a small group ahead of us shifted positions to take more pictures.

I stared at the door a minute longer. "Do you think this is an ancient equivalent of a *welcome* mat or a *no solicitors allowed* sign?"

"I couldn't say yet," Kate replied. "But welcome mats are more often than not found with decorations or signs."

"Maybe we came to the back door."

Our conversation must have gotten Dr. Fenton's attention. He was part of the picture-taking group, and now he approached us. His mouth was obscured by something dark, and I realized only when he reached us that he was wearing a filtering mask. "Put your masks on," he said, pointing to the equipment supply bin that had ridden in on the rails. "We're going to be boring a test hole soon." His voice sounded nasal.

Kate showed me where to find the masks. As we were putting them on, a loud voice echoed down the tunnel, warning everyone else about the same thing.

As we watched, workers set up a large drill mounted on a heavy base. One of the workers set a few controls which I imagined controlled drilling distance and force.

"Why not just try to open the door?" I asked Kate.

"Precautions. At least one archaeological team lost several members because they opened a vault that happened to be filled with water."

I thought about the entire butte being filled with water and how much larger the tunnel would be when it quit draining.

Finally the drill started. The crew had positioned the bit near the center of the door. They drilled much more slowly than I would have guessed, perhaps because they were cautious. I couldn't even detect progress as I watched.

After ten minutes I learned why. The drill hadn't penetrated the surface. When they pulled the drill out of the way and looked at the surface of the door, all they could see were faint lines. They wiped at the surface, and the lines of dust came away. Even under close examination, the door's finish was as smooth as a telescope mirror.

That caused as much furor as I expected, and after a delay they rolled up a large cutting laser to the door. They positioned it at an angle to the surface and I readily understood why after they had finished the first trial. When we were told it was safe to come back into the work area, we could see a red spot in the center of the door. It slowly darkened to match the rest of the door and when Kate pointed I could see the hole in the tunnel wall where the bounced beam had cut deep into it. The door itself looked as good as ever.

At that point, Dr. Fenton decided it would be a good time to adjourn and discuss the matter.

V.

Dead on Arrival

It was the next day before drastic measures were employed. By this time, I well understood the enormity of the departure from standard practice. A more typical method of exposing an artifact is to blow loose particles of dirt away with forced air. This time, they had an ugly, tight-focus, heavy-particle gun aimed at the door and had returned enough of the tunnel dirt to form an enormous barrier behind the device.

Kate and I felt nothing from several kilometers away, which was just fine with me. The technicians had spent a long time with the calculations and the monitoring equipment and had assured Dr. Fenton the device would shut off under any of several conditions indicating significant progress. I trusted them the way I would trust a grinning three-year-old with a gun. Maybe less.

When we got back to the tunnel, the cleanup crew had most of the dirt cleared out. We waited tensely for the underground people to tell us it was safe to come in.

This time we walked into the tunnel without the benefit of gas masks. The analysis said that no dangerous gases were present. I almost wished I had a mask anyway. The dust was so thick in the air I probably ate my childhood kilogram of dirt just by breathing on the way in.

Dr. Fenton led the party. Kate and I were with him. Sam Lund was there, too, along with another half-dozen archaeologists.

Near the end of the trip, we had to climb over a pile of rubble to continue. From there on, the formerly smooth tunnel floor was covered with fallen rocks. Most of the rocks were splattered with drops of sealer formed when the underground crew had sprayed the damaged ceiling with protective foam.

When I first saw the door, I thought it had survived the blast. But then I got closer and realized that what had seemed to be uniform flat black was really flat black sections at various distances. The door had an irregular hole punched through it, and beyond it lay a wall apparently made from the same stuff. The internal walls had suffered damage, too.

Dr. Fenton went through the opening first. Moments later, Kate, Sam, Fenton, and I were standing inside. Rummel Hurdt and several of the archaeologists cautiously waited just outside the opening. I hadn't appreciated Kate's rank around here until recently.

I felt slighted. Everyone but me had a belt pack.

"This is incredible," Dr. Fenton said in a hushed voice.

I agreed. The interior walls hadn't been as strong as the door, even though they seemed to be made of the same stuff. Several of them had been tossed violently away from the explosion center, and through one gap we could see a corridor leading into the distance. The corridor went so far we couldn't see its end.

But the really amazing part was that the corridor was lit. I scratched the base of my spine to get rid of a sudden itch.

Kate and I caught each other's gaze before we looked around near us. Sam Lund moved out of the room, and called to the rest of us, "You'd better have a look at this."

We all moved around the corner, into the larger adjoining area which had been crushed by the explosion.

Sam pointed. "It looks like you'll even have actual bodies to analyze."

Sure enough. Near the far side of the area lay a body. And going by the obesity, it looked from here like a Womper body.

Sam said, "Dr. Fenton, do you think there might have been a plague in here a long time ago? Something that could preserve a body like that?"

I moved toward the body, too curious for much caution. I stooped beside it and made a startling observation.

"I think you can scratch that theory, Sam," I said. "There's freshly dried blood here. This person was killed in the last hour or so, almost certainly by our explosion."

8

Open and Shut Case

I.

Forewarned Is Forearmed

As the implications of what I had just said sank in, I found myself surrounded by people. Kate, Sam, and Dr. Fenton all looked disbelieving.

Dr. Fenton was the most incredulous. He frowned and looked at me out of the corner of his eye. He made me think of a parrot. "That's impossible. This room has probably existed for ten thousand years. If anyone were alive in here—"

"Dr. Fenton, with all due respect," I said forcefully, "this fellow here died recently. Womper blood oxidizes when it's spilled into the atmosphere. Blood coming straight out of the body is brownish. Over a period of a day or so, it slowly changes to almost a pure white. This blood here is only partway through the change. And—" I rose and scraped my foot in the small pool of blood. Below the lightening surface was darker blood. It was shiny, obviously still liquid.

I rolled the body onto its back. It definitely looked like a Womper male, quite obese, prominent jowls, larger around the waist than the chest. Of his six fingers, the middle two were longer than the others. The Wompers I knew had fingers all close to the same length.

"I think you'd all better come over here for a minute,"

Sam Lund said softly. He motioned us around a nearby corner.

In the remains of the room beyond lay at least three, maybe as many as six more dead Womper bodies. It was hard to get an accurate count because the force of the explosion had ripped the room apart. Parts of bodies littered almost the entire room. It could have been a butcher-room sale at a sleazy organ bank if it were just a little neater.

Dr. Fenton was obviously stunned. For a long moment he moved his lips, as though trying to talk but failing. All his years of exploring long-dead sites had apparently done little to prepare him for this. Even I was taking too long accepting it all as fact. We were standing there, no doubt in various stages of numbness, when a voice called out, "Dr. Fenton? Sam?"

As a group, we turned toward the voice, and Sam called, "In here."

It was Rummel Hurdt, the Venton guard who had been stationed at the door. Zeldon Tal was with him. "We've got to get out of here fast," Rummel said breathlessly. It must have been serious to get him that excited. Zeldon's large eyes seemed to grow even bigger as he saw what was in the room with us. I wondered how he might feel about us just having killed several members of his race.

"What—" Sam started.

Rummel said, "Now! Fast! The hole in the door is sealing itself."

We ran. Or at least everyone but Dr. Fenton ran. He still seemed to be in shock, so I carried him. But none of us was in time.

The hole was nearly down to shoulder-width across and shrinking so fast we could watch its progress without straining our attention spans. I didn't want to be the one to try jumping through and then being bisected because I got stuck. Apparently no one else did either. In fact, it was already too small to let Zeldon out. His Womper size kept him out of at least a few places that smaller bodies could slip through.

As we stood there and watched our exit shrink, I asked Rummel, "Why didn't you call us with your wristcomp?"

"I tried." Rummel gave me his toothy Venton grin. "No one was home."

Almost too late, I had a thought. "Let's jam something in there. Maybe we can keep it open enough to talk through."

Rummel and I grabbed four rods from the rubble and rammed them through the opening. "Use vibrations to talk," I yelled through the rapidly diminishing hole to those outside.

The six of us all watched as the hole continued to close in on the rods. Finally, with only quiet snaps, each of the four rods was cut in two and the ends on our side fell onto the floor, bouncing and sounding more like plastic than any alloy I knew of. The center layer of the wall had come together completely, and now the black substance was filling in the rest of the small cavity the hole left behind. I don't think anyone spoke until the wall was once again in its original state. If anyone did, I certainly didn't hear.

"Maybe there's a back door," I said. No one smiled, but Kate had recovered enough to glare at me.

"What do you suggest we do, Sam?" Dr. Fenton asked, apparently also recovering.

Sam looked at me briefly, as though debating whether to accept the role of chief advisor, and said, "I suppose we'd better figure out some way of protecting ourselves."

"And you, Ben?" Fenton said. "What do you think?" I wondered if he would continue the question with Kate, Zeldon, and Rummel.

"I'd have to go along with that. We've just blown our way into someone's home and killed several family members. If that were *my* family, I'd be irritated."

"I've got a needler," Sam said. "Anyone else?"

No one else did, but I overcame my squeamishness long enough to take a closer look at one of the nearby bodies. "I've got a gun now," I said, removing a nasty-looking weapon from the dead body.

In the next few minutes, Rummel found two guns, one for himself and one for Fenton. I retrieved another for Kate. It was a little moist, so I gave her the gun I had found first. "You should probably get one of these, too, Sam," I said. "They may be better than yours." Sam began looking.

A moment later, we all possessed guns. We probably had enough firepower to boil away a good-sized lake.

Rummel was checking the far end of the room when he called to us. "Hey. It looks like this one is still alive."

We started toward him, making our way carefully through the spilled blood and twisted bodies. Rummel lifted a heavy beam from the body he was near and then leaned toward the victim's head and started to talk. He used a smattering of Womper words, telling the injured Womper he was trying to provide help. I didn't think the languages would be similar after such a long isolation, but it was a more likely bet than his own Venton speech.

Zeldon moved forward then. Maybe he could do a better job with the language.

I was a little behind Sam as we approached. Just as I got close enough to realize the Womper was female, her arms snapped up and her beefy muscular hands gripped Rummel around the neck. Rummel's initial gasping noises cut off abruptly as the grip tightened.

Sam didn't hesitate. He aimed his new weapon at her head and fired.

I blinked in the instant that white light filled the room, and when my eyes opened again the Womper was headless and shiny brown blood was forming a pool where her head had been. In death, the hands around Rummel's neck relaxed, and he struggled free.

"Thanks," Rummel said to Sam. He had to say it twice because the first time the word just came out as a squeak. The second time, his voice was still a lot scratchier than Sam's. His face seemed even paler than usual.

"I told you they'd be irritated," I said.

We stood there for just a minute, looking at one another. Zeldon had adopted an intensity I hadn't seen in him before. Maybe he was angry at Sam for killing a member of his race. Or maybe he was angry with me for indirectly causing several deaths.

Finally Dr. Fenton said, "Killing that person was rather severe, wouldn't you say, Sam?"

Sam held out the Womper gun to Fenton. "You read that scale and tell me what you think."

I looked over Fenton's shoulder and came to the same conclusion he did. "It's set—set on the lowest setting," he said, sounding dazed.

II.
Looking for Trouble

I felt dazed, too. We were standing right where we were now because of me. And already nearly a dozen people were dead because of me, because of the actions I had set in motion.

Kate must have somehow known what I was thinking, because she put her hand gently on my arm.

I grinned weakly at her and cleared my throat, still empathizing with Rummel. "I think it's time we got out of here."

"I agree," Sam said. "But where to?"

"There has to be a way. We need to find out what controls this door or find another door. But if we stay here, the inhabitants sent in as a backup will find us and they may be inclined to fight. And, if our friends outside try to get us out, the logical thing to do is use another explosive. If we're still nearby, we could wind up just like these folks here." I gestured at the littered floor.

No one disagreed. As we picked our way back through the broken bodies, I noticed that although the outside wall had resealed itself, the interior walls weren't endowed with the same capabilities. At least part of the damage we had done to this ten-thousand-year-old complex was going to have to be fixed the hard way.

We got to the edge of the damaged area and found ourselves with a three-way choice. We stood at the junction in a corridor that ran parallel to the face of the building we had broken into. At right angles to it, a hallway pointed straight into the center of the building. It was so long it dwindled to a point.

"I wonder why no one else has shown up," Kate said.

"Me, too," I said.

"Should we stay together?" Dr. Fenton asked, looking first at one corridor and then another.

I looked at Sam and nodded. He said, "Both Ben and I think we should. That leaves only the question of which way to go."

Fenton looked relieved.

"This way?" I said, pointing toward the center of the building.

"That may be the most risky," Sam said, "but it seems the way that gives us the best odds of finding out how we can get out. What do you think, Zeldon?"

"I would agree." Zeldon's eyes still seemed even larger than usual. His round face looked less cherubic than normal.

Fenton inhaled and then exhaled noisily. "All right. Let's try it."

As we began walking, I said, "I'd recommend everyone set the weapons at minimum. We all saw how much damage they did just at that setting."

The corridor was wide, nearly ten meters from side to side. The black surfaces of the floor and walls absorbed sound so well that I heard no echoes of our footsteps as we walked. The complex was a little like an enormous office building except there were no signs or decorations on the walls. About fifty meters into the corridor, we came across two doors, set opposite one another on the sides on the corridor. Neither had an obvious lock, but simply a push-plate.

"Who wants to be first in?" I asked. "Maybe we can learn something here."

No one seemed eager, so I asked Dr. Fenton, Zeldon, and Kate to flatten themselves against the wall on either side of one of the doorways. Sam and Rummel did the same but closer to the door. From just to one side of the door, I pushed it with my toe. It moved a few centimeters before I gave it a hard shove, and it swung open.

The door knocked heavily into an interior wall and stayed there. The room was dark, but only seconds later I realized it was beginning to brighten. I waited long enough to be sure of seeing well inside and then moved quickly around the corner, my gun ready.

There was no one inside. The room appeared to be an enormous storage area. I called to the others to follow me.

For as far as we could see clearly, there was a regular pattern; compartments about a meter high and two meters wide were stacked from the floor to a ceiling far above us. Built-in ladders were mounted next to every other column of compartments.

"What would they be storing?" Dr. Fenton asked.

"Let's find out," Sam said.

We approached one of the bottom compartments. From up close, we could see an inset, sliding cover. With the rest of us behind him watching intently, Sam slid the cover away to expose the contents.

Inside was a Womper, lying on his back.

"Holy Mother," Sam said, sliding the cover back rapidly.

No one said anything more for a long moment, as if everyone was afraid of making any more noise. Finally I said, "I don't think we need to worry about waking him up. He's in the big sleep."

Sam looked at me curiously.

"I think he's in suspended animation. Everyone in this bay must be."

"But there must be hundreds of these compartments in here," Kate said. "You think they'd have that many people in a state like this?"

"Either that or they're all dead or they're all just sleeping." At random, I opened five other covers and found five other plump Wompers, all on their backs. I left the last cover open for a moment. "This guy must be sleeping really soundly if he's not dead or in suspended animation. And look at the condensation inside."

Dr. Fenton put his hand flat against one surface. "If it's as cold in there as it looks, they've got an incredible insulator. This doesn't even feel cool."

"They're dead or suspended," I said. "And this just doesn't have the feel of a burial vault to me."

Zeldon didn't think so either.

"OK," Kate said. "But why?"

"No idea," I said. "Maybe we'll find out while we're searching for the door controls."

The room across the hall was just like this one. Back in the main corridor, we continued our search. Shortly we came across another set of doors. Both of those rooms were also filled with nothing but suspended-animation chambers, as were the next two along the hall.

"This is absolutely incredible," Dr. Fenton said softly, making a last survey of the room we had just explored. "Do you think this entire complex is nothing but frozen bodies?

And why would they do this? Why suspend so many people for ten thousand years?''

Sam said, ''I don't think we can answer those questions at this point. Right now I'm a lot more curious about why Wompers were awake near the door.''

I said, ''Maybe they woke up 500 years ago to go to the bathroom and couldn't get back to sleep.''

Rummel grinned and said, ''Yeah. Insomniacs.''

Dr. Fenton didn't give any indication he'd heard, but rather went back to the door and peered into the corridor. ''Don't you think we should keep moving?'' he asked.

As we walked along the corridor to the center, I thought about all those suspended Wompers. There must be thousands of them—millions if the trend continued.

III.
Where Do You Think You're Going?

Only a few minutes later we arrived at an intersection with a corridor that joined ours at a right angle. In all four directions now were hallways so long they dwindled to points in the distance. I felt a little like I was in an amusement park, looking at a series of mirrors that gave a similar illusion to a far smaller place. On the whole, I would rather have been in an amusement park.

I used the edge of my foot to make a mark on the wall near floor level. It would be easy to get lost in here. ''Anybody want to start a map?''

Kate volunteered. She pulled paper out of her belt pack and started writing.

''What else do you people have in those kits?'' I asked.

Fenton opened his and gave me a quick inventory. ''Camera, label tags, measuring gear, markers, brushes, a knife, a small air blower, a position marker beacon, a lamp.''

''No food?''

"No."

"Is the marker beacon always transmitting?"

"No. Just when it receives the command to."

Good. It wouldn't be broadcasting our location to the natives here, and it might be useful if our friends on the outside succeeded in getting in.

"How about taking a left turn here?" I said. "We can turn toward the center when we get to a hallway parallel to this one, and keeping out of this main corridor might make us harder for the natives to find."

No one disagreed.

The cross corridor was virtually identical to the first. We got tired of cautiously opening doors simply to find more cubicles. The hallway was a uniform black substance with seamless curves where the walls met the floor. I think the ceiling would have looked the same except it glowed brightly enough to make comfortable lighting. I didn't spend much time wondering how a black surface could glow. It looked as though someone had stretched a thin sheet of black cloth between us and a distant bright light.

"We still haven't seen anyone else awake," Zeldon said after we explored still another cubicle bay. "Could we have killed the only ones awake?" He kept his gun ready all the while.

I said, "Maybe others are waking up right now, but they're just not morning people."

Dr. Fenton drew in a deep breath. "Ben, would you mind trying to take the situation a little more seriously?"

"I am. You can't judge me just by what I say to lessen the tension, because I'm also thinking. For instance, have you thought about food?"

"Food? No. It seems a silly time to think about eating."

"Maybe. Maybe not. But it occurs to me that we're trapped in an enormous box. There may or may not be food stored where we can get access to it. If we're lucky enough to avoid any more hostile Wompers, it may still take us a few weeks to find out how to open the door, and we could starve by then. At the very least, we have to have a modest supply of water. So if you see a drinking fountain, let me know."

We walked another ten meters down the black, sound-absorbing corridor, and then Dr. Fenton turned to me and said, ''Point taken.''

At the next corner I noticed vertical decorative strips of adjacent circles set into each wall. We turned toward the center of the complex, having seen nothing other than more cubicles. I had a nagging thought that there might not be *anything* in here except more cubicles, but the theory made even less sense than what we had seen so far.

''Do you think it's possible that someone is tracking our progress, seeing which way we go, and preparing to come after us?'' Kate asked.

I looked at Sam to see if he wanted to guess. He didn't. I said, ''It's certainly possible. Since all we've seen so far are cubicles, they might even just watch us until we get close to something different, or until we do any more damage. That assumes a fair amount of restraint, but they may think our weapons are more advanced than theirs.''

''If they think that,'' Rummel said, ''they can't be as smart as we think they are.''

Sam said, ''So if we wanted to get their attention, we could destroy a cubicle?''

''I'm not sure that's the kind of attention we need right now,'' I said. ''If people are monitoring us, they might have had time to calm down and realize the only way we could get in involved force. But now we're in, if we don't do any more damage, they might decide we're peaceful.''

''Yeah, but are *they*?'' Sam asked.

''You're still thinking about the Womper who grabbed Rummel? You might have done the same thing in her place, half-delirious with pain, someone having just blown a hole in your living room wall.''

Sam stopped and spread his arms. ''Yeah, but why all this? Why all these Wompers in cubicles? It doesn't seem innocent to me.''

''Maybe there was a plague and they had to construct this to give the doctors time to find a cure,'' I said.

''Ten thousand years to find a cure?''

''Maybe they didn't work weekends. Maybe they had government-insured medicine. I don't know. Anyway, what do the words 'innocent until proven guilty' mean to you?''

''They mean taking needless risks.''

"That's what I like about you, Sam," I said. "You don't have any of those complicated philosophies to bog you down. I bet you don't subscribe to that save-the-children-first trash, either."

"These are our lives we're talking about here. We can't afford to walk right up to the next Womper we see and say, 'Awful sorry about killing those six on our way in. Let's talk about it.' If we let a hundred of them surround us, we'll probably never get out of here."

"That may be true, but when it comes right down to it, *we're* the ones in the wrong. If the only way out for us is to kill a hundred of these people, maybe we should lay down our guns."

"But I still say *they're* the ones in the wrong," Sam said. "This installation doesn't look peaceful to me. I think they've been hiding for a reason, not just because they like privacy. What do *you* think, Zeldon. They're your people."

"These are not my people any more than they are yours," Zeldon said. "If they have been in here for ten thousand years, I'm baffled. I think we should be careful. Beyond that, I don't know what to do."

Kate said, "Ben, are you suggesting we just put our guns down and wait for them to come for us and let them make the decision for us?"

"No. I agree with everyone who says we have to be cautious. I'm not prepared to surrender unless I'm convinced we've broken in on an entirely peaceful colony with no hostile intentions toward us. I agree, too, that there could be some sinister reason for these people to be in hiding. I just don't want to assume that and base all my actions on it without proof."

"Well," Sam said. "I hope we get your proof while we're still alive."

"I'll work at it real hard, just for you."

"You do that, because if someone shoots at me, I'm shooting back. In fact, I'm changing the setting on this to the highest."

"Go right ahead. For all I know, the guns are booby-trapped so if an outsider sets it to the maximum the gun explodes. Or maybe it will fire only once at the highest setting."

Kate said, "You don't really think that's a possibility, do you?"

"It doesn't seem likely. I'm just tired of people making assumptions."

That seemed to squelch the conversation, so we walked in silence as the black surfaces sucked up almost all stray sounds of our feet on the floor. In the distance we could see another intersection, but we stopped to investigate one more door. Beyond lay even more cubicles with Wompers in suspended animation. I hadn't seen so many stiff, lifeless bodies since I was in school.

In the next room we came to we tried an experiment. I called out on my wristcomp to Kate in the hallway. It was no good. The walls must have been incredibly good insulators in the wrong section of the spectrum. Or they were very good conductors—I couldn't remember the course in school.

We continued down the corridor. I reached the next door ahead of the others and opened it cautiously.

"Oops," I said. "Excuse me." I backed out of the door and let it swing closed.

I looked at five startled expressions and said, "Just kidding."

Kate glared at me.

We reached the intersection and Sam peered around the corner. "No one," he said. "Just another long, empty corridor."

This intersection was also decorated with vertical strips of circles. When I noticed Zeldon looking at them, I wondered if perhaps they were functional. "Traffic monitoring?" I asked, coming up behind him. "Visitor control?"

"I have no idea."

Although most of the disks were glossy black, one of them near eye level was brown. I ran my finger across it and felt nothing. "I wonder why only the one is brown," I said, rubbing the one above it to see if it felt any different.

I felt myself jostled from behind. I turned to see who was doing it, but no one was there. A transparent, glowing plane cut off the path down the corridor, isolating me from Dr. Fenton and Rummel. The plane felt solid. I kicked at it, and it seemed as unyielding as the real walls.

Sounds of surprise from behind me made me turn to see what else was happening. In each direction the corridors were cut off by glowing walls, boxing in me, Kate, Zeldon, and Sam. "Can you hear me?" I yelled back at Fenton.

He obviously saw my mouth move but he shook his head to indicate he couldn't hear what I was saying. The wall turned opaque at the same time the other three did.

"What in Mother's name is going on?" Sam said.

I had no idea, but at least we could hear each other. Only seconds after Sam had spoken, the floor lurched under us and my legs bent. Kate steadied herself. We were rising fast.

"It's going to crush us," Sam yelled as we passed the halfway point to the ceiling.

I crouched, not thinking at all about how little good that would do. And then the ceiling passed through us. Or we passed through the ceiling. It could have been one of the holograms in the university chart room for all I felt as I penetrated the plane of the ceiling. About the same time my head passed through the plane, the floor below us slowed dramatically, obviously keeping just a little behind gravity. I never left the floor, but for a long moment, I couldn't have walked anywhere because I felt as though I were falling, the floor below me falling just a bit slower.

I came down off my tiptoes, and my body lurched a final time as the floor stopped moving beneath me. The walls started to turn transparent again, and I said, "Next time maybe I'll take the stairs."

9

Hot on the Trail

I.
Am I Getting Warmer?

I put my finger on the trigger of the Womper gun I had confiscated and leveled the weapon in the direction of the elevator wall nearest me. The glowing plane continued its transition to becoming transparent and nonexistent.

"Each of you pick a direction and get ready to warn the others if you see anyone," I said. "We might have landed right in the middle of things."

They all responded rapidly. Kate had the wall to my left, Zeldon was on my right, and Sam covered the rear wall.

The residual glow faded into nothingness, and no one said a word. I was facing another long, empty corridor, and when I turned I saw everyone else was, too. Several seconds passed before I remembered the floor I now stood on had moments before been no more substantial than a hologram.

The level we were on looked identical to the one we had started out on. If it hadn't been for the sensation of rising, I could have believed that we were exactly where we had been, but that Dr. Fenton and Rummel had disappeared.

"We'd better get back to the others," I said. "Shall we try this again?"

Kate said, "Give me a second to let my stomach settle. It'll probably be worse on the way down."

"We'd better not wait too long. It could be that anyone using the elevators sets off an alarm."

"Let's go," Sam said.

Kate nodded.

Zeldon seemed not at all bothered by the sudden acceleration. He said nothing but stood guarding his direction.

I pressed the brown disk, not sure if that was the main floor or the floor we were on. Nothing happened. I pushed the disk right below it. Still nothing.

Sam said, "What's the problem?"

"I don't know. Maybe they're standing in the intersection and this thing won't move unless there's no one in the way." I pressed both buttons several more times.

Kate said, "Maybe we should get out of the intersection in case they're trying to follow us."

"I don't even know if they saw me push the button, but we can do it just in case." I stepped out of the square formed by the intersection and stood in the hall. So did the others. We waited impatiently for three minutes, but no one used the elevator.

"Try again?" I said finally.

The others walked back into the square. Again nothing happened when I pushed the brown button, but the one below it got action.

The glowing planes reappeared, cutting off the corridors. As Kate had guessed, the trip down was rougher. The floor fell almost fast enough to make me think we were in free-fall, leaving me teetering on my tiptoes, trying to pull myself toward the floor. No sooner had my stomach decided to cooperate than the elevator slammed to a halt with such force that Zeldon was the only one of us left standing when the journey ended. It was almost as bad as jumping off a small building and landing with nothing to break your fall but a pedestrian.

I struggled to my feet, watching the wall fade and trying to see if Rummel and Dr. Fenton were on the other side. They weren't.

But in the distance was a Womper running toward us, gun ready.

"Stay put!" I yelled, scanning the other three directions.

Sam said, "Holy Mother."

Our friends were nowhere to be seen. I punched another control disk. The walls stopped disappearing and reformed. An instant later the rising floor crushed itself against my feet. As we rose, my ankles suddenly grew painfully hot. A second later the sensation was gone. The Womper's weapon must have been able to penetrate the wall. At least the wall had cut the weapon's strength.

"Everybody OK?" I asked as soon as we passed through the ceiling above us.

A "Yeah" from Kate and two grunts from the others said that at least the four of us were all right. But what about Fenton and Rummel? I hoped they had started running when they saw the Womper approaching. Maybe our arrival would split the Womper's attention and slow him down. Rummel should be able to do as good a job as anyone at protecting Fenton.

"Sam, pick a direction to run when we get to whatever level I pushed."

"We can defend ourselves against one Womper easy enough."

"Fine. You stay here. Everyone else get ready to run with me this direction," I said, pointing at the wall closest to me. "If he's down there he probably knew where we were from the elevator activity. But this time he could have gotten another thousand people after us. It's a chance we don't need to take. And in case you don't remember, he was firing at us without our firing at him."

I flailed my arms as our ascent slowed. I couldn't actually tell if my feet were touching the floor for at least five seconds. I must have hit a button several levels higher than where we had been last time. Only luck kept me on my feet.

I gave Kate a hand to steady her. As the field responsible for the walls died, Zeldon came close, obviously ready to run with us. Another black, empty corridor showed through the diminishing glare. The other three directions were empty, too.

The wall finished disappearing, and we ran. After several steps I realized Sam was running with us. Zeldon surprised me by keeping pace easily. I hadn't thought much about

Wompers running before, but just assumed that all that bulk would slow them down. I guess if you've got the right muscles and motivation, you can make any body move fast.

The walls on this level did just as good a job of silencing our movements as the lower ones had. Zeldon could have been an underweight dwarf for all the vibrations his pounding footsteps generated.

This floor was different in at least one respect, though. The doors along the hall were set at wider intervals.

"How far?" Sam asked, panting.

"At least past the next intersection," I said. "We don't want to make it too easy if he followed us up here."

As we neared the corner, Zeldon ran ahead to see if anyone was in the corridor perpendicular to ours. He gave us a crisp all-clear sign, and we took a right turn.

"If we just stay in the corridor, we make good targets," I said. "Let's try a door."

We tried the second door on the left. As usual, the lights came on automatically, but at least this room wasn't filled with cubicles.

II.
Turning the Tables

Beyond the door was a room larger than the cubicle bays and even stranger.

A large, curved track ran around the room, in places coming within about a meter of each wall and in several other places curving in toward the center of the room so far that it almost touched itself. At apparently random intervals, the track was suspended from the floor by a variety of bizarrely shaped supports each large enough that they seemed to be doing far more than merely holding up the track.

The track was about the width of my hand with sides only as high as the thickness of my hand. It was nearly level with my waist. In the center of its surface were what appeared to be silvery ball bearings approximately the same size as a human eye. They moved along the track as though on an assembly line in a factory, except they traveled quite slowly.

Quite a few of the supports were large enough to conceal a person. "Take cover," I said. "As far from the door as you can. I see another door in the back. Maybe we can get through there."

The others moved away fast, and I stayed near Kate. "What the hell is this place?" she asked, dodging a speckled, blue-green support that wrapped around the track in a vertical, many-layered spiral.

I moved around one that looked like an orange tuning fork that didn't even touch the track. "Unless this is the way candy is made, I don't have a clue."

Near the center of the room, both ends of the track turned vertically into the ceiling. The section of the track coming down held dull lumps of what looked like putty. Going up, the spheres sparkled brilliantly and appeared flawlessly smooth. I passed by a solid-seeming cube that the track traveled directly through. Maybe it used the same tricks as the elevators.

Sam and Zeldon found concealment behind two of the larger tray supports near the rear of the room. I had started for the rear door to see where it led when Sam called to me. "Wait a minute. Why are we running?"

"So we don't have to kill anyone who's after us. And so they don't kill us." I backed away from the door and kneeled behind another support, a blue one that rose all the way to the high ceiling.

"There shouldn't be too much worry about anyone killing us. There are four of us, all armed. They have to come in here after us." Sam's voice was even scratchier than normal, no doubt because of the exercise.

"Except that for all you know they have a display with them showing what lights are on in these rooms, and they can turn a switch to evacuate the air in the room we're in. If we can stay away from them while they're in a shooting mood, maybe we can find out how to use the internal communications system to talk to them so they can't shoot at us until they've heard what we have to say." I couldn't believe it. Here I was arguing to use the comlink instead of talking in person.

"That's assuming we can say anything they'll understand,"

Sam said. "Zeldon, have you seen anything in here you've been able to read?"

"No. I haven't seen anything in writing."

Sam said, "You wouldn't be just saying that, would you? I mean, these people are like you whether you say they're your people or not. You wouldn't be thinking about siding with them, would you?"

"Sam!" Kate said, a frown on her face. "That's the most asinine thing you've said in a long time. Zeldon is with us. He's always been with us. He wouldn't desert his friends any more than you would."

Zeldon blinked his large eyes. "Thank you, Kate."

"You agree, don't you, Ben?" Kate said.

"I don't know. How long is a long time?"

Kate glared at me.

"Oh, I agree about Zeldon being with us. I was just trying to figure out how long it's been since Sam said something asinine."

Now Sam glared at me. Great. Kate, Sam, and an irritated Womper somewhere nearby. Zeldon was the only one who hadn't frowned at me lately.

"Well, if we're going to stay in here and wait for them, we'd better be prepared," I said. "Sam, get behind that red pillar in the corner. We need someone in a position to give us more leverage if negotiations don't go smoothly."

As Sam moved away, I ran to the back door to make sure it was unlocked. It was. Beyond it lay another strange assortment of machinery, or whatever it was, similar to what was in the room we were staying in.

I regained the cover I had picked earlier. "Zeldon, watch the back door so no one surprises us there, OK?"

Zeldon nodded solemnly and turned toward the rear, his gun ready.

"No one shoots unless there's no possibility of negotiation," I said. "Is that understood?"

Kate nodded immediately, followed by Zeldon. A moment later, Sam said softly, "Agreed."

Since there were no echoes, the instant Sam stopped talking, the room turned quiet. Besides the thumping of my heart, there was only a low-pitched hum from the contents of the room. I wondered what the equipment's purpose was. It could just as easily be a playroom as anything functional.

I was still trying to figure out a likely possibility when the door we had come in through was knocked open and slammed against the wall. I peered around the corner of my hiding place. The doorway was empty.

"Call to him, Zeldon," I said, just loud enough for him to hear. "Tell him we mean no harm. We didn't know anyone was alive in here, and we just want out. Use the oldest language you know."

Zeldon's voice was ragged as he spoke the first few words that were unfamiliar even to me. He paused. When no response came from the hallway, he spoke several more sentences.

Still there was no response. Zeldon shrugged his shoulders and turned back toward the rear door.

"What now?" Kate asked from her hiding place. "Do we just wait?"

"If we wait long enough," Zeldon said, "There will be time to get reinforcements."

I said, "Give me a minute. I'm not sure what's best—"

"What in Mother's name is that?" Kate said.

I followed her gaze. Floating in through the open doorway, about waist high, was a silvery object about the same size and shape as a water glass on its side. It rose and fell with the air currents, but generally strayed no more than a hand's width from its original height. At first it slowly rotated horizontally, as though someone had gently spun it before letting it go.

The cylinder end pointed briefly at me, swung in Kate's direction, past her toward Zeldon. Finally it completed a full circle and stopped rotating. And one end pointed at me. I ducked behind my cover.

"It's coming toward you," Kate said. "Let's get out of here!"

"No!" I said. "That may be exactly what they want."

There was silence for a moment and then Kate reached around her hiding place, aimed her gun, and squeezed the trigger. There was a crackling sound like air being ionized by lightning.

"It didn't do a thing. But now it's heading for me," she said. Her voice had a shake in it I hadn't heard before.

We could have run for the door behind us, but I was even

more wary of that way out now. The open door in front of us, coupled with this floating whatever it was could easily be part of an effort to flush us the way the hunter wanted us to go—maybe out the door we had come in through. Or the hunter could easily be right behind the rear door.

That gave me an idea. I leveled my new gun at the rear door and squeezed the trigger for a quarter second. Aside from the crackling, there wasn't much to see or hear. I squeezed the trigger again, this time for a full second. A wide circle on the door began to glow.

I peeked toward the floater. It traveled slowly, but I was convinced it had turned slightly and was now on a course for the rear door. Good. It must be heat-sensitive.

"This involves a risk," I said, "but keep something between you and the floater. And watch the front doorway, but I don't think anyone's there. I think he's behind us now."

The spot on the door began to fade, so I gave it another burst to keep it glowing. The floater continued on its path toward the door, and we slowly crept around our respective hiding places.

I should have covered my ears. When the floater finally reached the door, there came a loud and powerful explosion. It was so strong the floor under me vibrated and my ears began to ring. Trying not to take my gaze off the front doorway for too long, I glanced toward where the rear door had been. Not only was it missing, but a sizable, semicircular section of the wall around it was gone, too.

III.
Go Ahead. Make My Day.

On the other side of the damaged wall lay an injured Womper. He was reaching for the weapon that had obviously been knocked out of his hand in the explosion. The gun lay no more than a half meter from his head. Before his fingers touched the gun, a crackling noise sounded again, and a violet beam aimed from inside our room severed his arm and took away part of his head. Sam pointed his gun vertically and then jokingly blew across the top of the muzzle.

"That's real funny, Sam," I said. "Now there's one more person who can't tell us what's going on in here."

"He wouldn't have told us anything. He tried to kill us. He either ignored what Zeldon said to him, or he didn't care to find out."

I couldn't argue with that. "Skip it. Just cover that door while I search him. Kate, you and Zeldon keep watch for anyone else out that way." I pointed through the arched opening into the adjacent room.

Although the wall had been destroyed in a semicircle at least three meters across, the floor directly under the explosion was littered but intact. I wondered what it would take to damage the floor. As much as it took to get through the outer wall?

With the other three on guard, I kneeled beside the partly vaporized Womper body. He had four pockets, each just above his waistline, two in front, two in back. Rolling him over took a lot of energy. In the back left pocket were five silvery papers that looked like candy wrappers. I decided they must be dormant floaters. Not knowing how to activate them, or how to control them, it was probably safest just to leave them where I found them. Instead, I took them.

The Womper wore nothing like our wristcomps. For all I knew, they submitted to cranial implants, but even if the whole head had still been there, I wouldn't have explored. There was nothing else in the pockets and nothing in the way of jewelry or decoration. Just the one-piece, long-underwear-like clothes, functional boots, and the gun. Dressed to kill.

And now he was dead. And I hadn't the slightest idea if he was simply zealously protecting his homeland or had taken enjoyment from hunting us. In either case, he would enjoy nothing again.

"We shouldn't stay here too long, should we?" Kate asked, breaking me out of my useless chain of thoughts.

"No. Let's get out of here." I picked up the Womper's gun as the others regrouped around me.

Something about the gun was different from mine. I held mine and his up together and saw what it was. The muzzle on mine was twisted. His had a straight, white line on the underside of the muzzle. I twisted mine so the two white lines came together and pointed it at the wall. When I pulled the trigger, instead of a spot a half-meter across starting to glow on the wall, a tiny hole the size of a coin turned incandescent before it melted through.

"Focus," I said.

"Ben, are we going or not?" Kate said.

I looked back at the Womper body and I realized what other thought had been nagging at me. "One thing first. Zeldon, I need you to do something here."

Looking puzzled, Zeldon came toward me.

"Help me get him out of this suit, will you?" I kneeled next to the body.

Zeldon stopped about a meter from the body. "What do you want to do that for?"

"I'm a necrophiliac, what do you think? Protection. Hurry, will you? If you're wearing his suit, the others might think he caught us. It might buy us a few crucial seconds."

"You can't be serious. Put on that suit?"

"Don't worry. We'll turn our backs. Come on. Help me."

"But I don't think—"

"This is vital, Zeldon. You heard me talk about how simple lack of water can eventually kill us. Well, we could die a lot sooner than that if one of these guys catches us when we're vulnerable."

Zeldon started to help me, patently unhappy with the turn of events.

It was distasteful work. Fortunately, the suit was short-sleeved. If it hadn't been, there would have been one long sleeve and one ragged sleeve. The material was strong. In our haste, we pulled at it fairly hard, but it didn't tear. The seam that run up the front of the garment was virtually impossible to pull apart by tugging in one direction, but when I tried a different grip, it parted as easily as a smooth zipper but with no sound. Rolling the large, inert body was the difficult part. This guy was even heavier than Zeldon. The stump of his half-vaporized arm was probably as big around as my neck.

Finally, we rose, Zeldon holding the suit but still obviously reluctant.

"Do it," I said. "Put it on over your own clothes if that helps. Your sleeves look shorter than his, so they shouldn't show."

Zeldon nodded and slowly began to pull on the dead man's suit.

I widened the beam of my gun and stretched my arm far enough from my body that the beam shouldn't hit my feet as I played it over the dead Womper's body. The body began disappearing rapidly, but the stench was terrible. I also had campfire syndrome; each time I repositioned myself, the fumes came directly at me.

By the time the body had been incinerated, Zeldon was into his new outfit.

"It's you, Zeldon," I said. "Very chic."

Zeldon actually frowned at me. This lack of appreciation was getting tiring.

"That may save our lives."

Zeldon nodded grudgingly.

"Well," I said. "What are we waiting for?"

IV.

I Love a Mystery

Rather than go through the room where the dead Womper had been circling around behind us, we left via the way we had come. At least we were sure no one else was hiding in the room we had been in.

There wasn't anyone in the hall, either. I started to go to the left when Sam said, "Don't you want to keep going toward the center?"

"Yeah. That's why I turned this way."

"You're turned around. The center's that way," Sam said, pointing to the right.

"What do you two think?" I asked Kate and Zeldon.

Kate shook her head. "My map isn't much good since we started running around up here."

Zeldon said, "Either way is acceptable, as long as we turn

that direction at the next intersection.'' He pointed back into the room we had just exited.

''You're saying the center is *that* direction?''

Zeldon nodded.

''Come on, Kate. Give it another try. This won't be completely symmetrical unless you balance out Zeldon.''

Zeldon said. ''I'm quite positive.''

''OK. We go with Zeldon. Any problems?''

Sam shrugged.

Kate said. ''Let's do it.''

''Right. Zeldon, you watch our rear for right now. Ah, let me rephrase that.''

''I know what you want.''

We reached the intersection without seeing another native, and we turned left to take us in the direction Zeldon guessed. The walls at the ends of the corridors in all four directions were far enough away that I couldn't tell which edge of the complex was nearest.

We zigzagged again, passing still more rooms apparently filled with manufacturing equipment. We continued along the next hall.

''Good news and bad news, huh Kate?'' I said after we briefly explored one more room.

''How so?''

''This may be the biggest find of your career. And if we're not lucky, we might not live to tell anyone about it.''

''Don't try to cheer me up.'' Kate's lips looked thinner than usual.

''Why haven't we seen more Wompers so far?'' Sam asked. He was guarding the hallway to our rear now.

''Maybe we've killed everyone who was awake already,'' I said bitterly. ''Pretty awesome performance, huh?''

''I keep telling you, it's them or us,'' Sam said.

''Yeah, but I keep forgetting.''

Two hallways later, we cautiously opened yet another door. Beyond it lay an immense room full of equipment like nothing we had seen so far.

After convincing ourselves there were no native Wompers to notice us, we walked through the door and then sideways along a catwalk fastened to the wall. My acrophobia switched itself into overdrive. I found it difficult to think about things other than the depths below us. After a moment of staring, I realized that I had backed up flat against the wall.

"It's enormous," Kate said softly.

It was. The far walls might have been as distant as the next intersection was, so the "block" we were in might have consisted of only this one vast chamber. What was even more surprising was that the room extended easily six levels below us and rose maybe eight levels over us. Catwalks traveled the perimeter of each level, and grilled stairs led from one level to the next.

In the center of the chamber, starting from the bottom level and rising all the way to the ceiling far above us, were two immense concentric spirals. Each spiral was flat and wide, so a person could start at the bottom and walk all the way to the top if he had a long enough attention span.

Both spirals were loaded with obstacles to walking, though. As though someone had turned them into bizarre parking strips, each spiral supported an enormous number of vehicles or something about the same size, all parked bumper to bumper, or front to back, or nose to tail, or whatever to whichever.

The builders had done a reasonably good job conserving space; not much more than a hand's width over the top of each craft, the next level of the spiral wound its way upward. At intervals of five crafts, there was a space just wide enough for an overweight Womper to squeeze through. Through those spaces, we could see that the inner spiral carried a similar load. Between the two spirals was a spiral catwalk.

A bewildering array of colored outgrowths from the walls and floor touched the spirals in numerous places, the outgrowths reminiscent of the tray supports in the room we had been in earlier. Again I thought of a manufacturing center. Catwalks accompanied most of the many-colored, oddly shaped constructions.

"What do you think those are?" Sam said, obviously meaning the objects on the spirals.

"I think we can probably rule out amusement park rides, but beyond that I have no real idea. Shuttles, skimmers, some kind of craft?"

"I've got an idea," Kate said. "If the natives tracked our use of the elevator to find out which level we were on, we could walk down to another level and get off there so we'd be harder to find.''

It was a good idea. The part I didn't like was the part about walking along those catwalks, but the others agreed it was the best course of action. Moments later we were moving quickly and quietly along one wall, suspended at a height great enough to make a dropped shoe lethal to someone walking on the floor.

I kept telling myself the odds of my slipping and spinning over the guardrail were lower than the likelihood of my having a cardiac arrest right then, but somehow the odds of a cardiac arrest seemed higher than I had ever thought them to be. We continued on the walkway as I thought about bad jokes involving terminal velocity.

10

The Heat Is On

I.

Fall Guy

I could see straight through the grated catwalk, all the way to the next level below and beyond it to the next level below it, and still—

"Are you all right, Ben?"

I glanced up to see Kate looking at me with a concerned expression on her face.

"Fine. Fine. I just get a little queasy around heights."

"We could blindfold you so you didn't have to look." Kate obviously didn't take this as seriously as I did.

"No. That'll be quite all right. Thank you very much for your suggestion, though."

"Any time." Grinning for almost the first time since we got inside, she turned her attention back to the path ahead of her and walked faster to catch up with Sam and Zeldon.

We had reached the halfway point on the wall we were on when Sam said, "You know, if someone catches us when we're like this, we'll be easy targets. If we use the catwalk between the two spirals out there, we could always duck behind whatever those things are."

I looked at the walkway leading out to the spiral. Except for being perfectly level, it wasn't vastly different in concept from a vine footbridge out of some ancient jungle melodrama. And it ran straight into the center of the hall without benefit of having a wall running next to it. I wondered if Sam was sensing my discomfort and getting back at me for the jokes I'd made.

Kate and Zeldon both agreed it was a good idea, so we departed from the catwalk against the wall and began our way out to the spirals. The railings on either side of the catwalk were single bars, about waist high, supported at infrequent intervals by rods of similar size.

We reached the edge of the spiral without mishap, although I was slower than the others.

"What's the matter, Ben?" Sam said. "It isn't *that* far to the bottom."

"I'm not sure exactly how far it is. How about if I drop you over the side and time your fall?"

"Stop teasing him," Kate said, apparently forgetting how recently she had done the same thing. Maybe everyone likes to find chinks in other peoples' armor. "Lots of folks are bothered by heights."

At the edge of the spiral, the catwalk formed a "T." The tilted crosspiece ran just level enough to match the slope of the spiral and extended for about the length of three—three "tanks" I decided to call them. There was a gap between the one on our right and the one farther down the spiral, so we stepped over the rail and onto the spiral. I felt a lot better on the spiral than I had while I was getting to it. Zeldon had a tight fit getting through, but Sam and Kate had a comfortable margin.

I stopped to look more closely at the "tank" as I passed it. The tank was vaguely shaped like an armored passenger craft, the outer layer made of a black substance that could easily have properties in common with the outside walls here. There were, however, no wheels, treads, hover jets, stubby wings, or any other indication I could see that the tank was actually intended to travel under its own power.

The bottom was rectangular, with rounded corners. About halfway up, the sides tapered into a rectangular top of about half the area of the bottom. At each top corner was a small bump. As I looked more closely, I could see patterns on the matte black surface. None of the patterns seemed to overlap another, and most were rectangles and circles at various points on the skin.

I ran my fingers over the surface. The tank seemed smooth to the point of feeling oily, but when I took my hand away and rubbed my finger and thumb together they were as dry as before. "Now that I think about it," I said, "I don't know that I've ever been in a cleaner place. There hasn't been any dirt at all in here. If these people had good enough dust detectors, they could probably just track us by our footprints."

"I'm glad you're feeling better," Kate said. She had waited for me when she realized I dropped behind. "Did your parents drop you when you were little?"

"Not that I know of. I don't remember anything happening to me to trigger it. Maybe it's just my heightened sense of self-preservation at work."

"Maybe it does work. You *are* fairly well preserved."

"Your sentiment is overwhelming."

"Are you two coming?" Sam whispered loudly to us.

Kate joined the other two on the spiral catwalk that hugged the inside of the spiral we were on. I followed.

From here we got a good view of the center spiral. It seemed to be carrying a load similar to the one we had just left. The only difference was that, since it was smaller, there were fewer tanks on its surface. The scene was so eerie that for a while I forgot about looking down.

Sam had begun descending on the catwalk. The three of us followed cautiously, the others probably as awestruck as I was. Every tank we passed looked exactly like the one before it.

"I wonder how often it moves," I said finally.

"How often *what* moves?" Kate asked, glancing over her shoulder.

"The spiral. I don't know if it's moving continuously but very slowly or if it moves just once in a while."

"What makes you think it moves?" Sam asked.

"The catwalk on the outside. It had the crosswise section. If this thing never turned, they could have just built catwalks that led straight out to the openings between these tanks."

"Tanks?" Kate said.

"Or whatever they are. They feel like weapons to me."

Sam said, "I thought you were convinced everyone in here was a newborn innocent."

"You probably thought that because you didn't listen too well. All I said was I wanted to keep an open mind."

"Would you two argue less and cooperate more?" Kate said. "We've got enough troubles."

"I'll try this again," I said. "I guess I'm beginning to lean toward Sam's side."

Kate said, "Because of what happened back in that room? Because he was sneaking up behind us?"

"Yes and no. Sneaking around is common sense when you're not sure what capability the enemy has. What got to me was the floating bomb. That thing obviously caused a lot of damage, and it might have done even more if it had gone off next to the contents of the room. It's like someone using a rocket launcher on a housebreaker. Even someone like me might eventually figure a person who overreacts like that may be desperate, willing to do anything it takes to finish the job, not bothering to think about the consequences."

"It's about time you figured that out," Sam said.

"I'm not saying I'm ready to blast every native on sight. I'm just saying I'm more suspicious than I was."

"At least you're getting closer."

We continued down the spiral catwalk. I felt better having the bulk next to me. The others were silent for the time being. Aside from the muffled sounds of feet against the grate and the soft rustling of several pairs of pantlegs in motion, the cavern was quiet.

I examined the tanks as I walked. On this side, too, each unit had fine lines etched into its surface. Apparently etched, I should say; when I ran my hand over the lines, I could feel nothing except a continuous, impossibly smooth exterior.

After passing several more units, I realized the lines weren't the same on each. They must have been customized, or numbered, or something out of my realm of knowledge.

I watched the patterns as I made my way farther down. Only after I had passed another dozen units did I realize there was a common element in each pattern. On each unit, there were two horizontal parallel lines near the top.

I stopped where I was and looked at one set of lines more closely. At the same moment, I remembered the zipper-like opener on the Womper's suit. I ran my finger across the lines and felt nothing. I ran my finger along the length of the two lines, first in one direction and then the other.

A panel on the side of the unit swung silently open, almost pushing me off the catwalk. I regained my footing and peered quickly inside. Maybe it *was* a tank or something equivalent.

Abruptly I looked back at the others. They were continuing down the catwalk, apparently oblivious to me. With almost no conscious thought, I swung the panel closed. It fit into place with a *snick*.

"What was that?" Sam asked, turning.

Zeldon turned almost at the same moment.

I tapped my fingernail against the unit next to me. The door was machined to such a tight tolerance that the seam was invisible. "Just kicking the tires."

Sam had turned around even before I thought consciously about concealing my discovery. Zeldon was slower to turn back to the path ahead. Kate and Zeldon could probably deal with the fact that we might have access to a powerful weapon, but I wasn't so sure about Sam. If he knew, he might insist on blasting the place apart while we looked for the control room. And, for all I knew, these things might not be functional anyway. They could be in the middle of some incomprehensible manufacturing stage.

That hadn't been the impression I got from the view inside, though. The control panel had been lit with a soft red glow. A single seat, large enough for a Womper, was centered in the vehicle. And I was sure it was a vehicle now. Although the outside of the sloped front looked as black as the rest of the surface, it had looked transparent from the inside.

I was catching up to the others when Sam cried out, "Holy Mother!" He sounded as though he was in pain.

II.

Drop It!

With my gun ready, I scanned every direction, trying to see if the Wompers had caught up with us. I saw no one.

Sam seemed to be fumbling at his side. An instant later, I saw a glowing, red, marble-sized sphere drop from his hand. It hit the catwalk and bounced over the side.

The sphere fell, glowing still more brightly as it did, shifting from red toward white. By the time it was halfway to the floor it was as bright as looking at the sun except it was a lot smaller. Impossibly, it grew even brighter as it dropped farther. When it reached the floor, it was hazardous to look at.

Fortunately it hit something on the floor that deflected it, and it rolled out of our direct line of sight. Even that wasn't enough to make it totally safe to keep our eyes open. As it rolled and bounced, shadows came and went, as though an arc welder were being waved around no farther than ten meters away.

"What was that?" I asked.

"Are you all right?" Kate asked.

"Let's get out of here," Sam said. "I'll explain later." He began to run down the catwalk, stopping at the first gap between tanks and moving rapidly between them. The rest of us followed as fast as we could.

I hurried through the space, following Kate. Running along the catwalk out to the wall was almost a religious experience, but I made it without tripping and falling over the railing. The reflected light was so bright that the entire room seemed lit, including what used to be shadows. I felt like I was in a foundry.

From the side, we ran to the nearest door. We must have been two levels down from where we had come in, but for all I knew we were going back in the direction we had come from. I just wanted out. The air temperature had risen several degrees since we had started running, and I was sure it wasn't just my metabolism.

The hall outside was deserted and felt noticeably cooler. Zeldon pointed in the direction he thought we should go and that was good enough for me. My legs felt a whole lot better than before as we ran along the corridor.

Two corridors later, Sam was about to open another door, when I said, "Maybe we shouldn't hide in rooms. We might be just as safe near an intersection so we have several ways to run."

Sam backed away from the door and we ran to the next corridor.

"Are you going to tell us what happened in there?" I asked as we stood there recovering from the exertion.

Sam waited for his breathing to slow down. He brought one hand up to where we could see it. On his middle two fingers were several spots where the skin had whitened and smoothed as it would with a burn. "When we were in that room, the one with the tray traveling around, I got curious about what those spheres were," he said between big gulps of air. "I touched one and it was loose in the tray, so I decided to take it and look at it later. I put it in my back pocket. You know most of the rest. While we were walking down that catwalk, I felt this burning heat against the back of my leg."

Now that he pointed, I could see the scorched area at the bottom of his pocket outline.

"I managed to get it out of my pocket, burning my fingers at the same time. And you saw how hot it got after that. So now I've got burned fingers, a burned leg, and I still don't know what that thing was."

"Well, it could have been worse," I said philosophically.

"How do you figure that?" Sam asked, frowning at me.

"You could have put it in your *front* pocket."

Sam grimaced.

"You know, I never really saw you as a kleptomaniac before," I said.

"Blow it—"

"Gentlemen, gentlemen," Zeldon said. "I hate to interrupt your discussion, but I think we may have a visitor coming."

III.
I Thought We Took Care of You

We looked in the direction Zeldon pointed. Almost too far away to be seen against the black background, a dark shape traveled silently toward us. It was hard to be sure of the size, but it was probably about a quarter the size of the tanks we had seen earlier and roughly the same shape. About two intersections away, it came steadily toward us.

I turned to Sam and said with an overly serious tone, "Now see what you've done."

"Come on, you guys," Kate said. "It's time we did something."

"Which way do you want to run?" I asked.

"Run?" Sam said.

Zeldon said, "I think Ben's right. It may be hostile."

"At the risk of being too obvious," Kate said, "maybe we should run *away*."

"I like that," I said. "Anyone object?"

I didn't give anyone a chance to say anything more. We were probably all feeling a little cocky after having stayed alive this long. "I want to do an experiment. Zeldon, you run that way." I pointed ninety degrees away from our approaching friend. "Kate and Sam and I will run that way." I pointed 180 degrees away from Zeldon's course. "When we all get to the next intersection, wait for it to see all of us and find out who it follows. Zeldon's suit may be protection of some sort. Turn that way when you start running again, so we can double back and meet again."

No one disagreed so we all started running. I liked to keep fit maybe even more than the next guy, but this wasn't my idea of fun exercise.

Bad news. The thing following us traveled almost as fast as we did while we ran. Not long after we reached the next intersection, it arrived at the one we had just departed. Kate and Sam stood to one side of the intersection so whatever that thing was would be comparing only two factors: Zeldon and me. It paused, motionless for less than a second. When it started moving again, it was heading for me.

Somehow I didn't have the feeling it was just cleaning the floors.

We ran down a corridor at right angles to the one we had just been on. We really were doing a lot of running lately. Sam must have thought so, too.

"Why are we running?" he asked between breaths. This was probably harder for him than for me. "We don't know for sure if it's hostile."

Kate said, "I'm not *that* much of a gambler. How do you propose to find out without taking a big chance of getting blown away?"

Good question. Sam continued running without responding.

We got to the next corner and turned toward where Zeldon was. In the distance, he was running toward us.

"Go on ahead," I said to Sam and Kate, stopping just around the corner. The device hadn't showed itself yet. I spent a few seconds wondering whether I should just run after the two of them, and hope the thing would lose our trail, but I had to get more information.

There. It had reached the corner and turned toward us. I leveled my gun at it and pulled the trigger. A crackling in the air and a hazy violet beam were the only indications that the gun had discharged. The thing behind us certainly didn't slow down.

I ran toward the other three. I caught up with them almost at the next intersection. From the sound of Sam's breathing, we had to find a solution fairly fast.

"Run that way," I said, pointing back toward the way we had been coming from before we saw the thing traveling toward us. Once we were running along the corridor, I said, "Zeldon, you and Kate and I will get halfway to the next intersection, and then start checking every door we pass, to see if we can find another room with more than one door. Sam, you just keep going straight ahead."

Zeldon said, "Right," and the other two nodded their heads.

The first door I tried was no good—just more cubicles. Kate and Zeldon had no luck either. The next several doors were negative, too. By the time we got to the next intersection, we had found nothing. An instant after we got there, our follower reached the intersection behind us.

We took a left and started concentrating on the doors on the right side of the hall. Still nothing.

We tried more doors, and finally Kate yelled, "This one, back here!"

We backtracked and found ourselves in a room full of empty tables and benches and things that looked like sinks. It was a cross between a school chemistry lab and a warehouse. We didn't stop to look at the scenery, though. Zeldon and I moved two boxes in front of the door, jamming them between the door and a bench that looked to be mounted on the floor. Then we made straight for the rear door where Kate and Sam were waiting for us.

The room beyond looked similar, and it had a door on the far side.

We waited at the doorway, having a couple more boxes ready to use to force it closed, too. The wait was a short one. Only seconds later, the door we had come through bumped open wide enough to get a hand through and then hit the cartons blocking it. The door swung closed.

Nothing happened for another second, and then the door bounced against the boxes again, harder. This time one of the boxes seemed to be crushed on one side, but the door opening was still too narrow for a person to squeeze through, even a human.

A third blow struck the boxes, but they didn't seem to get any worse this time. A short wait followed.

"Maybe it's given up," Kate whispered.

"And then again, maybe not," I said. Now a bright line was forming on the wall next to the door.

We watched the burning outline as it proceeded to cut about half of what would surely be an opening for the device to travel through. The line looked so regular, I was sure that when the section on the wall fell inward and the device rolled in through the opening it would clear the edge by no more than a fingernail thickness on each side.

IV.

Hot Pursuit

We blocked the second door and started running again.

There was nothing available to block the door back to the corridor, so I turned my gun on the seam of the door and gave it enough heat to fuse the door to the wall. Maybe that would force our follower to cut through the wall again. At least that would slow it down.

So now we were back out in the hallway. I hardly knew which way was which anymore.

I turned my palms up and then pointed arbitrarily in one direction.

Sam and Kate were obviously ready to go when Zeldon said, "If I may offer a suggestion, I think this way might be better."

"You've got it, Zeldon." If he was willing to speak up and suggest an alternative, he probably felt far more strongly about it than I did, no matter what the topic.

We followed him down several corridors, moving more slowly as time went by.

Finally I realized where we were going. "This is where we were earlier, right, Zeldon? The spirals."

"Exactly. If we were to go back in on the catwalk, it might follow us. If someone were to stand just to one side of the door, maybe that person could push the thing, whatever it is, over the side. The guardrail is too high to help it."

"Are you volunteering, Zeldon?"

Zeldon didn't reply. We had plenty to think about, so I didn't spend much time thinking about him.

We were fast approaching the right place. This had to be the hallway we wanted because of the spacing of the doors. I halted the others at a door about halfway between intersections. With my foot, I edged the door open and bright light streamed out. Warm air flowed through the gap.

I said to Sam, "That sphere you took is going to revolutionize the heating business—maybe not on Tankur but almost everywhere else."

I pushed the door open farther. The air was hot, but probably not as hot as a sauna. We could live in there for a reasonable time as long as it didn't get too much hotter too fast. The familiar catwalk ran both directions against the wall.

"Kate, Sam, head that way," I said. "Zeldon, you follow them."

"I can be the one to try to knock the thing off." It was Kate who volunteered, not Zeldon.

"I appreciate the willingness, but I think this is a case where we need all the physical strength we can get." Still Zeldon didn't volunteer, so I turned Kate in the direction Sam had started in and gestured to Zeldon to follow her. "Stay on the catwalk at least until that thing gets here."

Kate looked at me a long moment before she began to run.

I stepped through the door, and I felt worse than I would have in Dallad heat. After no more than ten seconds, I found myself hoping the thing would show up quickly. It was so hot it even took my mind off the height for a moment. I looked straight down through the gaps in the grating, and the sight didn't even bother me.

The spirals in the center of the room looked just the same as they had before except the lighting was brighter.

I stood there, trying to think what the best method would be. Standing behind the door would give me more protection, but the door might interfere with my trying to push the thing over the side.

I shouldn't have thought about being pushed over the side. It took a moment for my head to stabilize. But when it did, fortunately I had a better idea.

The catwalk was mounted against the wall at about body-length intervals. I walked to the support just to one side of the door. With my gun focused as tight as I could make it, I cut through all but two of the running strips in the grate. The slits hardly showed.

I didn't want to walk back over that stretch now, so I backed up and took a running jump across the weakened section. My heart pounded as I thought about slipping on landing and then falling off the catwalk. Or having the thing arrive and opening the door exactly when I was in midflight.

I landed on the stable side and expelled enough air to blow out a birthday cake for a ten-thousand-year-old man.

On the other side, I made more cuts in the grate. When I was finished, I pressed my hand hard against the weakened section. It didn't give at all. That was strong stuff. I cut halfway through both remaining supports, and it felt the same as before.

I didn't know how much more to cut. If I took away too much, the catwalk would just fall. If I didn't get rid of enough, I'd be invited to a cozy little get-together with our follower.

I cut away all but about a tenth of two gratings. I sure hoped that thing was as heavy as it looked.

There wasn't much else to do now except wait. I looked back at the others and saw they were safe. I was still surprised at Zeldon. With his enormous strength, he was the obvious candidate for the job. Had he volunteered, I might have argued briefly to be civil, but I would have given in.

Maybe I myself was a victim of generalizing. I didn't remember meeting a Womper yet who didn't seem to have an overdeveloped sense of self-sacrifice and a duty to please others. Their largest religion had a monumental emphasis on guilt and confession. But that didn't mean Zeldon had to be the same way.

It must have been hot enough in here to boil blood. Mine sure felt that way. I couldn't tell if it was hotter now than when we came back in or not, but the sphere somewhere on the floor far below still seemed to be sending off enough light to leave radiation shadows behind when it was gone.

I wished the sphere were gone. I wished *we* were gone. I wished the thing would arrive.

One out of three isn't too bad. The door beside me bumped open.

As the door swung closed again, it hit an obstruction. Our follower had nosed into the doorway. Slowly the door began to open again, shielding me from the follower for the time being.

The door continued opening until it was straight out from the wall. Why didn't the grate give way?

The nose of the follower appeared beyond the edge of the door, and for the first time I had the sudden dread that it could hover or even fly if it had to.

Kept in the Dark

I.

Did Anyone Get The License Number?

I stood there, my back to the wall, sweating profusely and unsure of what to do next.

Why didn't that thing fall? The follower was almost all the way onto the weakened section of catwalk, and the catwalk had creaked. Maybe that thing could fly, or it was on a hover cushion of air. But it was silent—no ground-effect vehicle I had encountered before was silent. Maybe I would have to try to push it over the edge after all.

Its nose extended farther past the edge of the door. I moved.

Hanging on as tightly as I could to a support on the wall, I brought one foot down fast and hard on the edge of the weakened section.

Nothing.

But then there came a *snap* like someone breaking a dry tree branch, and the end of the weakened section of catwalk lurched down about the width of a hand.

Hopeful, I lifted my foot to kick again. I brought it down hard and almost unbalanced myself to the point of falling, because at that same moment, the section gave way completely and wasn't there when my leg extended. The grate started to fall.

Our follower fell, too. The grating had tilted outward just before it came completely free. Now the device had a clear drop all the way to the distant floor below. I watched it, hoping it didn't have the power of flight. It tumbled for what seemed a long time and then finally hit.

I was so absorbed by it all that for the moment I forgot I was standing next to the edge of a precipice.

There was no obvious sign of damage when our follower hit the floor. It bounced, intact, finally coming to rest upside down.

I started toward the others and was halfway there when I heard a sound from below. The thing was righting itself. It must have had a flywheel it could gradually speed up and then suddenly stop or some more advanced ability, because as I watched, it flipped itself over and began roaming on the distant floor.

If we were lucky, it would get too close to the burning sphere. In any event, even if it was undamaged, it should take quite a while to get back to the floor we were on.

I joined the others and watched our friend below. "Too bad you didn't steal more of those balls, Sam. You could have circled that thing."

"Let's get out of here," was all Sam said. The heat seemed to have made his voice scratchier than before.

As we were walking the rest of the length of the catwalk to the door, Kate took one hand and gripped my upper arm. She squeezed tight enough to raise welts.

"I'm fine," I said softly. "Thanks."

The hallway outside felt like a walk-in freezer compared to the steamy, blistering cauldron we left behind us.

"Which way, Zeldon?" I said. "You seem to have the best navigation system."

Zeldon pointed. We walked.

"Ben," Zeldon said after a few dozen footsteps. "About what happened back there. I know that I should have—"

I didn't want him apologizing for not volunteering. I was irritated with myself for having expected him to anyway. "Zeldon, in here we've got to concentrate on the present and the future. Unless you saw something back there that we can use to increase our odds of survival, let's keep our attention on what's ahead of us, all right?"

Zeldon blinked his large eyes at me and then looked briefly straight ahead. "I suppose you're right," he said finally.

We rotated the job of watching behind us. For at least the first several minutes, the tail gunner was unnecessary.

"I wonder what's ahead of us now," Kate said. "We haven't seen any native Wompers for quite a while."

"Maybe that thing we left in the spiral room was the last line of defense," I said.

"Things are never that easy in real life, are they?" she said.

"You call this easy? You must have had some tough jobs before you got to be an archaeologist."

"No, but my sister had twin boys," she said innocently.

I looked over at her and despite the pressure she was grinning. "I wish Dr. Fenton were here to hear this. Does the archaeology handbook allow frivolity on the job?"

"It's not obvious to me that I'm on the job. This isn't really a dead city, you know."

"It may be by now," I said more grimly than I had intended.

I seemed to have this late-blooming knack for squelching conversation. We continued walking through those dark corridors, no longer bothering to open more than one door per hallway. There were still more cubicles and machinery of vague or unfathomable purposes.

Each time we passed through an intersection, I kept imagining that, like a lost pet accidentally abandoned far from home, our follower would suddenly emerge nearby. Except it would probably not be wagging a tail or feather, but rather taking aim. Instead, every hall looked as empty as the one before it: silent, uninviting, gloomy.

"Are you sure we're heading for the center?" Kate said at last. "It looks to me like we're coming toward a wall."

I looked far down the corridor ahead, and the vanishing point looked a little brighter than the other three directions did. "We couldn't have walked the length of the butte yet— not after circling around so much. How sure are you about directions now, Zeldon?"

"That is the center," he said, pointing in the direction we were going, toward the slightly lighter end point.

"I think we should continue," I said. "I can't explain it either, but Zeldon seems sure."

Sam said, "OK by me. At least we're walking instead of running."

As we traveled the length of the next two "blocks," it became more obvious that the hallway was taking us closer to either a blockage or the edge of the complex. The end of the corridor was distinctly lighter than the black surfaces we had found everywhere else.

Even before we reached it, the curvature was noticeable. In a place like this with so many flat surfaces, curves stood out like snowshoes on a dancer. Once we neared the end of the corridor, the extent of the curved surface was apparent.

From where we stood, there seemed to be an enormous sphere embedded in the complex. The cross corridor followed the gentle curve out of sight in each of the side directions. If it was a sphere, its diameter must have been even larger than one of the long "blocks" we had passed on our way. The far wall of the cross corridor bulged slightly and leaned toward us, indicating we were below the center line.

No one else seemed to want to talk, so I said, "Maybe this *is* the center. But where's the door?" The corridor halls against the curved side were unbroken.

Zeldon said, "Maybe they are level with the center—halfway up."

"So we should take the elevator up? That sounds reasonable to me."

"But we could be walking straight into their arms," Kate said.

"What choice do we have?"

Kate grimaced. "Going up?" she asked, reaching toward the strip of disks next to the corner.

The three of us nodded. She pushed the disk just above the brown one.

Again the field walls glowed, and again I had the feeling that I was on the very end of an orbital-insertion ride, subjected to the last seconds of heavy acceleration and the first few seconds of weightlessness as the drive cut off. The only difference was that this time I also felt lateral pressure, making it even more difficult to remain standing.

The field disappeared and we found ourselves pointing our guns at another curved blank wall.

"We've got to go higher," I said, seeing that the top of the wall still protruded farther than the bottom.

Kate pressed another circle. At the next two levels, we repeated our performance. The field died once again, and this time we were pointing our guns at a closed set of doors.

"There are doors all the way along here," Sam said.

I looked in the direction he had gestured. The wall of the sphere curved slowly out of sight, and at frequent intervals there were doors set into the wall. This level seemed to be crisscrossed with corridors, too, because at each door, a hallway led out from the sphere.

"I don't know about you folks, but I'm fairly curious about what's inside there," I said.

"Let's find out," Kate said.

Sam reached for the door.

"Just a minute," I said. "I think it would be safer if Zeldon held a gun on us. Let's us three stick our guns on our belts, around back if you can."

"I don't know if that's wise," Zeldon said. "We may need every second to defend ourselves."

"But there could be hundreds of Wompers in there. If we have to shoot our way out, we probably won't make it anyway."

"But—oh, very well." Zeldon gave in, but he certainly didn't look pleased.

Zeldon aimed his gun in the direction of Sam and Kate and me. He pulled open one of the two doors, and I got the other. We three humans held our hands over our heads as the four of us walked slowly through the doorway and into the slightly darkened interior.

II.

Signs of Foul Play

My eyes were still adjusting when Zeldon said to us, "Don't move!"

Less than a second went by before the crackling of his gun told me we had trouble. I backed slowly toward the wall so I would stand out less if I drew my own gun.

"I think we are all right for now," Zeldon said even before I reached the wall.

"What's going on?" Kate said. Sam's identical words echoed hers about a syllable behind.

My pupils finally dilated to the point that I could see the distant wall of what was indeed an enormous sphere—a sphere that seemed to be either a command center or a bizarre theater. To our left, at a lower elevation about a third of the way around the sphere, was what seemed to be the remains of a Womper body. That was the direction Zeldon had fired in.

Zeldon spoke slowly, keeping his face turned toward the direction he had been looking. "I had to kill two of the natives. They were drawing their guns, and I couldn't afford to take the chance." Despite the nature of the room, there were no audible echoes whatsoever.

I drew my gun. We seemed to be the only living people in this room, but it was so large and had so many potential places of concealment that it was impossible to be sure. The interior could have been a cross between a theater and a work of modern art. Several dozen horizontal rows of seats ringed the inside, the slight distance-caused blurring giving it a feeling of spinning. The rows were grouped in sets of four, interspersed with expanses of textured areas that served functions I didn't even guess at.

The rings of seats didn't actually circle the entire perimeter. At what I took to be the "front" of the sphere, the rows were broken by a curved gap of about a fifth of the circumference.

The oddest feature, though, was the set of four stalks. From the bottom of the sphere extended four long, thin tubes

that ran toward the center, stopping about two-thirds of the
way there. At the end of each stalk was a spherical pod. The
lengths of the stalks were sized so the four pods were level.

"This has got to be the place we can open the doors
from," Sam said. "But how?"

"No idea yet," I said. "Kate, you or Zeldon have any
guesses?"

They shook their heads.

"OK. How about if we each take a quadrant and work our
way to the bottom. Meet between the bottoms of those center
two stalks."

"Who goes where?" Kate asked.

"Why don't you start here? I'll take ninety degrees to the
left. Sam, ninety to the right. Zeldon, since you're probably
the strongest, why don't you take the far side?"

Zeldon hesitated before he nodded. Perhaps people were
leery of being separated even in the same room, but no one
objected. Kate started down a nearby ladder, and Sam moved
off in his assigned direction.

Zeldon and I started to the left. A walkway circled the
sphere, wide enough for ten people to travel abreast. At
frequent intervals there were doors to the outside and ladders
leading both up and down. The ladders going up didn't reach
too far, though. If they had gone much farther, the overhang
for the people sitting in those seats would be dangerous. Even
the seats at this level were contained in oval pockets cut into
the side of the sphere.

It was a long walk to the ninety-degree point. I kept my
bearings by looking at the line of stalks. "Why do you
suppose those people were starting to shoot at us, Zeldon?" I
asked as we walked.

"I don't know. Perhaps they were just quite cautious and
planned to shoot only you humans. Perhaps the concept of
taking prisoners is foreign to them so they knew I was an
impostor. I don't have any good explanation."

"You ever see anything like this in your culture before?"

"No. Never."

"I didn't think so. What about those pods?" I pointed.

"Possibly a place to command from."

As we walked, I occasionally noted where Kate was as she
descended. Her progress was slower than mine because she

had to contend with the ladders. Finally I reached the point where I was to start down.

"I can go down this way if you'd rather," Zeldon said. "That way you wouldn't have to pass those bodies."

"I think I can handle it," I said, swinging onto the ladder going down. "I'll see you downstairs."

"Very well." Zeldon moved off toward the side opposite the place we had entered.

I started down the ladder, still surprised that Zeldon was so often vocalizing his desires lately. I looked closely at the first pocket I came to. It was cut smoothly into the wall of the sphere and contained one Womper-sized seat. It also held a seat belt. I moved from the ladder into the oval area and seated myself. My body hardly filled the chair. Was the seat belt just insurance in case someone fell asleep? It would be a killing fall if a person were to slip out of the chair.

I stretched my arms and a light came on. I moved my arms back to my side, and the light went off. I looked all around for compartments that might hold materials that would give more clues to the room's function or the inhabitants' roles. Nothing.

One of these pockets could be a good hiding place. I looked at the far side of the sphere where Sam was traveling down a ladder and saw countless similar pockets, all dark. All, I assumed, were empty.

I got out of the chair and moved across a narrow ledge to the next pocket. It looked exactly like the first one.

Back on the ladder, I continued down. After passing many more identical pockets and chairs, I reached the level where Zeldon had shot the people. Here the strip was wider, broad enough for me to lie down on with my body pointing toward the center of the sphere.

Zeldon's blast had been messy. The floor was littered with sprayed bits of flesh and brown chips of wall surface. He must have set his gun on a much higher setting than I had used. I couldn't have said whether there had been one person here or four. The largest remaining chunk of a body wasn't much bigger than a shoe.

Some control panels near the scene had also taken a powerful hit. I wouldn't necessarily have known there were any controls here, but where Zeldon's beam had hit there was a long scar on the side of the wall, and it had curled up sections of things reminiscent of display panels.

I pulled a section loose and exposed an even more familiar outline. A sleeper cubicle. I wrenched it away from the wall, and behind it was another.

I took a good look through the cover and knew this sleeper would never wake. Maybe the person inside had already been in the process of reviving, or perhaps he had been still frozen down when Zeldon's blast severed power to the cubicle, but the person inside looked less like a Womper than a Womper-shaped mold of mud—mud that had once been wet and then had dried out under Dallad's hot sun, leaving behind a hideous dry, cracked surface. I shook my head and looked away, wondering when all the killing would stop.

I realized now that the entire surrounding area had been swept with high-energy destruction. Maybe Zeldon's hand had jittered.

Behind the second cubicle was another. All three were in the same state. Maybe this partially explained why we hadn't seen any other Wompers recently. We might have killed all those alive, and this was where more were being revived. If it took an hour or two to revive a frozen Womper, they might have just gotten up before we got here.

Terrific. They had been asleep for maybe ten thousand years, and when they woke up, we killed them. Can't I sleep for just a few more centuries, Mom?

For a long moment I couldn't get the euphemism "put it to sleep" out of my mind.

III.

Lulled Into
A False Sense of Security

Nearby doors led out of the sphere. Maybe we had been just one level above here when we first reached the outside of the sphere. Or the doors might not uniformly circle the sphere at all levels.

I looked across the sphere, and I could see Sam's tiny form continuing down. Kate was farther along. If I yelled, I might have been able to get their attention. I called Kate on my wristcomp.

"Are you OK?" she asked.

"Fine. I was just curious about whether these things work in line of sight in here."

"You certainly are a curious person."

I resumed my downward trek on the ladder. Below me, it gradually switched first to stairs, then a ramp, and finally the almost flat center of the sphere below that. There must have been an automated way to get down there, but I didn't see it, and I wanted to explore along the way.

There were enough seats and oval pockets in here to accommodate only a fraction of the sleepers, but that was still a sizable number.

When I reached the next strip between rows of seats, I found what looked like more controls of some kind. An alcove opening onto the center of the sphere contained two chairs in front of a sloping panel covered with bumps of various sizes and colors. In front of the chair at eye level was a rectangular outline on the wall, but nothing I pressed made anything change. Perhaps the power to this alcove was cut off, or maybe it was simply locked out until a full crew was in the sphere.

Nearby was another similar-looking alcove, and after it was another. The line might have continued completely around the sphere at this level. I tried unsuccessfully in two more alcoves to bring the equipment to life. Everything around here was dead.

When I went back to the ladder, Kate was nearly at the bottom, and Sam was almost as far down as I was. Zeldon wasn't in sight, but I didn't worry much about his taking care of himself.

The ladder began to lean more and more away from vertical, and finally I reached the end of it. Steep stairs with handrails continued downward. Gradually the steps grew wider as the height of the risers dwindled. I passed more alcoves of equipment, all of which were deactivated.

The ramp was more comfortable than the ladder and stairs

had been. Sam was near the bottom end of his stairs and coming closer.

Looking up at the ceiling gave me almost as strong a sense of acrophobia as I probably would have got by looking down from the top. It was an eerie feeling.

Kate was standing next to the base of one of the stalks as I approached.

"Find anything useful?" I asked her.

"That depends on how useful a bunch of lifeless equipment is."

"Same here. Maybe these things have the answer." I glanced up at the nearest stalk. About as wide as my outstretched arms, it towered above us like a flagpole over insects.

Sam joined us a few minutes later, and by then I could see Zeldon coming down the stairs. There was still no other sign of life in the sphere.

When Zeldon joined us, he could add nothing to what the other three of us had already seen. "Perhaps up there," he said.

We took a closer look at the base of the stalk. At first glance it seemed as smooth and black and shiny as the tanks we had seen earlier. I hoped the only way in wasn't to teleport from some other area in the complex.

It didn't take long to notice the parallel lines, though. Lines like the ones that had opened the door to the tank. I ran my finger along the grooves, and a door opened into the base of the stalk.

"How did you do that?" Kate asked.

I shrugged and showed her what I had done.

"What is this?" Sam asked, looking at the interior.

"This" was an empty, cylindrical volume with a ceiling not much higher than a person. I didn't know whether to be relieved or unhappy that there wasn't a ladder visible.

"Well," I said. "There's got to be some way up. Let me give it a try. But someone unlock the door again if I'm not out shortly." I stepped inside the cylinder and pulled the door shut before anyone could object loudly enough to stop me.

The darkness inside was absolute for a moment, but then a light came on, and a square panel lit before my face. So far I could have been in a refrigerator with the light wired backward. On the screen was apparently a sentence, but it was in no language I knew. I tried saying "Enter, open up, send me up," and a dozen other sentences in the oldest Womper dialect I knew. Nothing.

I saw nothing like a keyboard or a slot for a coded key, so I tried using my finger to write a few words on the screen. Again nothing.

I pushed on the cylinder surface where the door had been. The light went out, the screen darkened, and the door opened silently.

"No luck," I said. "Anyone else want to try?"

Kate and Sam nominated Zeldon, who might have a better chance than I did.

I told Zeldon what I had seen, and he took his turn in the cylinder.

No sounds emerged from the cylinder, but Zeldon took a lot longer than I had.

After about five minutes, Sam asked, "What's keeping him so long?"

Sam and Kate and I looked at one another, none of us apparently ready to guess what was happening. The silence lasted just three more seconds, and the cylinder door opened and Zeldon came out.

"It works," he said. He blinked his large eyes at me.

"What's the matter?" I asked.

"What do you mean?"

"I mean, I thought you'd look happier if it worked."

"I am all right. I just want to get out of this place."

"So do we. But we have to open the front door. Did you find out how to do it?"

"No. I just found out how to get up to the top. You speak the word 'lift' in an old dialect." He spoke a word that sounded nothing like the current pronunciation. "To go down, you just say 'drop' in the same dialect. He gave us the second word, and we all said them a few times until we sounded like Zeldon.

"Great," I said. "Is there space for all of us up there?"

"No. But I imagine we can each go up in a different riser. I think there is communication between them."

I started for the far stalk while Sam and Kate moved to the

two closest ones. At the base of the one I had selected, I opened the door and stepped into the cylinder.

I pronounced the word Zeldon had given me. Before my mouth had closed, the floor beneath me rose as fast as it had in the elevators. My knees flexed against the force, and the blood drained from my face. Fortunately, the builders must have designed the lift with a given acceleration in mind rather than a given force. If this thing had shot me up to the top with the same force necessary to propel a heavy Womper body, I would have splattered against the shell of the observation bubble.

If I had been feeling sick, I might easily have thrown up against the observation bubble. The floor slowed so drastically I was virtually thrown the last ten meters. At the height of my travel, just as I stopped rising and began to fall, a massive chair slid under me, catching me at the knees and scooping me out of midair. I hitched my trousers back up.

My head stopped spinning, and an array of blue lights on the interior console came into focus. Beyond them lay the view of the sphere. I was in the pod on top of the stalk, about a third of the sphere's diameter off the floor. On both sides of the array of lights lay touch panels with a dozen unfamiliar words on them.

"You are all in place satisfactorily?" came Zeldon's words clearly, apparently from the surface of the transparent bubble window in front of me.

"I'm here," Kate said.

"Me, too," Sam said.

"Present," I said.

Mixed in with the blue lights in front of me were a few green ones. Obviously these Wompers had a color code different from my own. I assumed the panel indicated most things, whatever they were, were OK, and a few things were not so OK.

"What do these words on the panels mean, Zeldon?" I asked.

"From the bottom right, visual, environment, support, security, that one I don't know, monitor, operations, inventory, status, communication . . ." He listed several more, each of which was less interesting than the first several.

"I'm trying 'visual,' " I said and put my finger over the last word on the right-hand screen.

In response, the entire surface of the sphere in front of the observation window lit up with an enormous rectangular panel of light. The speaker in my command bubble sounded two quick intakes of breath and two "ahhs" that must have come from Kate and Sam.

The screen was filled with groups of words and symbols, divided into countless small squares and rectangles with between two and twenty words per square. A few of the words seemed familiar because I was acquainted with the outside Womper language. Each word had a pictograph beside it. The pictographs didn't help me much. One looked like a snake that had been cut in two. Another showed an egg sitting atop a pretzel.

"Zeldon, what do you think—" I started, trailing off as I caught a glimpse of motion to one side of the screen.

"What do I think about what?"

"About the fact that we have visitors."

12

What Could Possibly Happen?

I.

Never a Dull Moment

"Where?" Kate asked.

"Over there," I said. "Near the bottom right of the screen."

"I don't see anything."

"Me neither," Sam said.

I knew I had seen something. "Well someone's there. I'm going down."

I spoke the word Zeldon had given me and the chair tilted forward. A second after my feet touched the floor again, the bottom dropped out of the world. I'd hate to use an escalator designed by these people.

At the ground level, my socks rolled down past my ankles as the tube stopped. I readied my gun. Staying in the chamber was too claustrophobic for a possible fight so I pushed open the door and moved quickly behind the stalk.

"We're friends," I shouted, loud enough to be heard anywhere in the sphere.

There was a moment's silence and then a surprised call came back. "So are we." The voice sounded like Dr. Fenton's.

"It's me—Ben," I called.

Fenton was more trusting than I was. He stepped forward into the light where I could easily see him. Rummel moved to stand beside him. They both had their guns in their hands. "We thought you might be dead," Fenton shouted.

"We're all fine," I said, moving out from the concealment of the stalk. "Come on down."

As they started down, the wall-screen image rippled through a dozen or so images and then went blank. Moments later, the other three with me had reached the floor and stepped out of their stalks. The four of us walked to meet Fenton and Rummel.

"I don't understand," Dr. Fenton said in a normal voice when they were close. "We haven't seen any other Wompers since you four vanished. We thought maybe you had been caught in some kind of trap."

"It only felt like it," I said. "It was just their equivalent of an elevator."

"An elevator?"

I explained.

"We didn't know. We just got away from there as fast as we could."

"And finally found your way here."

"Right. We kept moving toward the center, not having any better plan. Rummel seemed to think we could handle ourselves all right, although I must say I'm glad we didn't encounter any other hostilities."

"Yeah. You were lucky. Sam's been complaining all the way."

Rummel grinned. I was glad he was back.

Fenton took me seriously. "What's happened to you? At least you're all still alive. And why are you dressed like that, Zeldon?"

Kate told them the highlights of our trip. When she had finished, Fenton looked decidedly relieved that he'd been on the tame half of the journey.

"What next?" Rummel asked.

"We still need to find out how to get out of here," I said.

"That's already done," Zeldon said. "While you were on your way down, I found the controls for the door. It's now set for local control. When we get there, we should be able to open it easily."

"That's great!" Kate said.

It *was* great. That's why I was a little surprised that Zeldon didn't look happier, but I had learned long ago not to bet on what people are thinking just because of their expressions. And this wasn't over yet. There could still be some Wompers left awake.

I realized that by now I had come to accept Sam's assumption that the natives weren't too friendly. "Maybe we'd better move fast, as long as we're heading for the door. There might still be someone awake who could lock it again."

No one disagreed so we began to retrace Rummel and Fenton's path. They had never left the level we started on so that should have kept things simple. A little way up the side of the sphere, the six of us exited through the same door they had entered.

No one seemed to be relaxed enough to discard a gun, but the mood of the group seemed much calmer than it had been an hour ago. Unfortunately, I let myself loosen up too much.

According to Zeldon's directions, the door was a straight shot from where we were, so we started toward the outside. More out of curiosity than anything else, we kept opening occasional doors as we walked. After a few odd-looking rooms full of racks of equipment with lots of blue indicator panels, we started seeing mostly just more suspended-animation cubicles.

"We must really be the only ones awake in this whole place," Kate said after a while.

I said, "Maybe they missed their wake-up call."

We had traveled what I estimated to be about a third of the way out without incident when Sam called to me from a room up ahead. "Ben, take a look at this, will you?"

The others in the party had fallen a little behind us, strung out over about a quarter of the length of this block.

I caught up with him and entered the room he had called from. Sam was kneeling next to a cubicle. He rose and pointed at it. "Take a look. What do you think is happening?"

I bent over for a closer look. What had been frost on the inside of the transparent panel was now liquid condensation. I thought I could detect an odor I hadn't noticed with other cubicles. I leaned closer, puzzled. Before I could reach any conclusion, something sharp-edged and hard hit me just behind my ear.

I might have held on to consciousness for a portion of a second, no longer. My vision went black and I heard a rushing sound just before I passed out.

II.

Don't Try to Stop Me

"You're wasting your time," Dr. Fenton's voice said from somewhere behind me or above me or inside me. "That thing's coming straight toward us."

What thing? I wondered. And what had happened to me? I opened my eyes and the light streamed into my head, striking the back of my skull and bursting out the other side.

"Ahhhh," I said.

"He's coming around." That was Kate's voice this time.

"Good." That was Rummel's voice.

"Don't be too sure," I said or tried to say.

"Are you all right?" Kate's worried face was in front of my eyes the next time I opened them. The pain wasn't so bad this time.

"Fine. Never felt better. What in Mother's name is going on around here?"

"It's Sam. He's gone crazy. He knocked you out and took your gun. Then he took ours by threatening to kill you."

"This isn't making very much sense." I think I spoke clearly for the first time since the blow.

"Not to me either. He was going to kill us, but the thing following us showed up again. He must be planning on letting it do the job for him. It's getting closer and Sam left us here without any weapons."

Kate helped me struggle to my feet. Fenton and Rummel were at the door. Zeldon stood nearby looking helpless and dejected.

Fenton turned and said, "It's still coming."

I reached the door without my head leaving my body and pulled the door farther open.

"Watch out!" Rummel said. "He's got a gun trained on the door."

"You mean Sam?" I asked.

Rummel nodded.

"Sam what's going on?" I yelled.

"Don't play games with me," he yelled back. He must have been at the next corner because his voice sounded far away.

"I'm not feeling very playful. What's it all about?"

"Stop it, Ben. You knew about me and Elliot all along. I can't let you out now."

"What?" came from Kate and Dr. Fenton.

I thought for a minute, putting pieces together. "It's no good now, Sam. I already told my partner. If anything happens to me, he'll tell the police about you."

"Partner?" Kate said softly. "What *is* going on?"

"Nice try," Sam yelled back. "But I'm not that stupid."

I looked to the left and saw our follower approaching. This wasn't good.

I slammed the door shut. "Is there anything we can shove against this?" I asked, looking around wildly.

"Maybe you," Rummel said.

"Am I overreacting? You can tell me straight."

"You just haven't had time to adjust," Rummel said. "There's nothing in here that moves except us, and we won't be doing that for much longer. Sam shoots us if we leave. That thing cuts through the wall and puts us away if we stay. Do you have a preference?"

"Well, I'll be damned if I'm going to die without knowing why," Kate said angrily. "Are you going to tell us what's going on?"

"OK," I said. "Evidently Sam was Elliot's partner in stealing artifacts from your dig. I knew it couldn't have been a one-person operation. Not with the precautions you people took with the perimeter checkpoints. I teased Sam about being a thief when he took that sphere. He must have thought I had it all figured out and was just playing with him. After that, he couldn't let me out of here. Now he can't let any of you out of here, either."

Kate took a deep breath.

"We've got to move," I said. "Maybe we can squeeze

into some of the cubicles and make that thing think we're gone.''

"That won't fool Sam," Fenton said.

"One thing at a time. What's that?" I asked abruptly, pointing to a smoking pile of melted plastic in the corner of the room.

"Our wristcomps," Kate answered.

I moved to a cubicle on the bottom row. My head felt much better already.

The cubicle door was stubborn at first, but it gave way. The smell inside was worse than a pet store. I couldn't bring myself to evict the Womper body, probably killing it in the process, and there was no spare room in with it. I closed the door.

I whirled, trying to think of alternatives. Only one came to mind.

"What are you doing now?" Kate asked as I lay down on the floor, my feet toward the door.

"Blocking it. Someone get behind me. Put your feet on my shoulders. And someone get behind him. Fast!"

The edge in my voice probably helped get people moving faster. Zeldon lay down between me and the cubicles. Kate lay down with her feet on Zeldon's shoulders.

Kate said, "OK, push." I straightened my legs as the others did.

"Ouch, Zeldon. OK, I think we're all right." With our human door jam, the follower shouldn't be able to simply bump the door open. I hoped.

"What good does all this do?" asked Dr. Fenton. "That thing will just cut through the wall again."

"First of all, Doctor, I recommend you and Rummel get as close to the three of us as possible. The last time this happened, that thing started cutting to one side of the door. If you're unlucky, it could accidentally damage your clothes."

Fenton and Rummel moved together to the center of the room.

"Now, listen closely, all of you. If this thing is—"

The door bumped against the soles of my shoes.

"It's here," I said needlessly. The door bumped again, harder.

I went on quickly. "Since it's this close, Sam must have

backed away for his own safety, so he's not going to be an immediate problem."

"I'd like to know what an immediate—" Fenton began.

"Shut up! Now, once this thing"—bump—"starts cutting an opening in the wall, we're going to need a volunteer. Someone who can deal with a life expectancy measured in seconds. Since no one here qualifies, we'll have to draw lots. Quick, everyone guess a number between one and ten."

"Two?"

"Eight."

"Seven."

"What in Mother's name are you talking about?" Kate asked.

"OK. I was closest," I said. "When the—"

It started. A bright spot formed on the wall near the floor. An instant later it was a hole in the wall and it began to travel upward.

"Good," I said. "It's the right side. We can get up now." I did so. Staying clear of the cutting beam, I moved to the corner of the room. "Now, I stay right here. Come on, get up. That thing won't try the door again, not now that it's started cutting." The beam traveled farther up.

"Now I stay here. You wait next to the door. As soon as that thing starts in through the cutout, you slowly open the door, keeping it between you and the thing. As soon as it's inside the room, run like Mother."

"But that leaves you—" Kate started.

"It has to be one of us. Just do it."

"I'll do it," Zeldon said.

I looked at him for a moment. "Thanks, Zeldon. You do it next time."

Zeldon walked over to me, picked me up with his massive hands, and gently carried me, putting me down next to Kate and Rummel and Fenton who all stood by the door.

"Well," I said. "If you put it that way."

The beam had reached its high point and started down the final cut.

"Run fast and to the left," I said to the others. "Sam may not be all that far away."

The others nodded silently. The cutting beam neared the floor.

"Thanks, Zeldon," Kate said softly. Zeldon nodded.

The beam was almost at the floor.

"If you get separated," Zeldon said, "hide in the main control room. Sam can't corner you in there. Either he leaves the complex, and everyone else comes in, or he has to hunt you."

"Good point," I said. "And, Zeldon, one last question. Where is the spiral room from here?"

He gave the directions before he asked why.

I explained about the tanks.

The beam reached the floor. The semicircular section of wall stood freely, anchored only along the floor. The thing bumped once against the wall, and the wall slowly fell forward, forcing air aside as it dropped. I pulled the door in about a micron.

I took one last look at Zeldon. He didn't appear nervous at all. Of course, I couldn't ever tell what he was thinking anyway.

The thing edged its nose into the room, and I slowly opened the door to block its view of the four of us.

It moved farther in, and I opened the door wider. When it was halfway in, I pointed out the door and mouthed "go" to the others. Fenton and Rummel left together, moving fast. Kate and I followed. Unable to turn off my curiosity, I looked behind to see if Sam was in sight.

He was. And he saw us. Our only advantage was distance.

III.

There's Nothing More Dangerous Than a Wounded Detective

We neared the next intersection. I had to continue straight through to get to the spiral room. "Kate, you go right, and you, too, Fenton. Rummel, you go left here. All of you get lost."

At the intersection, we fanned out like stunt fliers, and I was left alone in the corridor with Sam coming after me.

Fortunately, he must have been slowed by the follower. I glanced behind me and saw only Sam—no follower. I didn't have time to figure out why.

I ran most of the way down the next block before heat flared in my legs. Sam was shooting now. I lurched, regaining my balance and avoiding a fall. Sam had followed me rather than any of the others. At least his gun wasn't focused tightly. Maybe he had left it the way it was when he melted down our wristcomps.

I reached the corner and made a sliding left turn. I was almost out of sight of Sam when pain lanced through the back of my arm. It caught me unprepared, and I lost control. I stumbled. I collided with the wall, hard, but I was out of Sam's view now. He must have got his gun focused finally.

I picked myself up and started running. When I hit the wall, I had banged my ankle hard enough to dent the wall, so it was tougher going now.

I considered hiding in one of the rooms, but Sam was coming fast enough to arrive in this hall before I left it, so he'd know immediately what I had done.

I ran, ignoring the pain as best I could. I was almost to the next intersection before Sam was in a threatening position again, so I was able to turn right without getting hit again.

This was where I needed to be. The spiral room was on my left. I pulled open the first door and raced into the inferno.

The white-hot sphere was still on the floor a few levels below. At first I was afraid the air was so hot I was scorching my lungs, but the worry diminished as I ran along the catwalk, still able to breathe. I marveled at my ability to run this way when the height bothered me. I wasn't as far off the floor now as I had been before, but I was sure the real explanation was that somewhere deep in my brain the priorities had shifted.

My feet thudded on the catwalk as I turned out toward the spirals in the center of the room. Vibrations traveled ahead of me and behind me. I was a perfect target right then, and I hoped that Sam might guess I went in the other side of the hall first, giving me another precious second or two.

A noise behind me sounded over the pounding of my feet. The door had opened. But I wasn't where I needed to be yet. I was still perfectly exposed.

A crackling noise by my ear told me Sam hadn't missed by much. And then I was twisting, scrambling to make my way between two tanks. A stripe of red glowed brightly just to one side of me and finally I was out of his line of sight. I ran up the ramp inside, not daring to pick the very first unit in case Sam could open it before I could figure out how to lock it. Then he could just parboil me and start looking for the others.

I picked the fifth unit and ran my finger along the parallel lines. Nothing happened.

I tried it again. This time I tried to calm down and do it right, moving my finger in a straight line. The cover opened.

The glowing red instrument panel softly lit the interior. I scrambled in, sinking deeply into the large seat. For a moment I couldn't touch the door. I reached toward it with my left arm and the pain chose that moment to flare again. I sat forward in the chair and twisted so my right arm felt the inside of the door. Finally I found a handle and pulled down.

The light from the opening shut off and my eyes readjusted to the view through the forward screen. The view to the outside seemed slightly dimmer than real life, as though the screen contained automatic brightness-limiting gear, and it was currently set to filter some of the bright light outside.

Sam wasn't far behind. He was just reaching the spiral as I watched. He passed through the gap between tanks and started up the ramp, not even looking at the first two units. He had obviously seen which way I had gone. He looked intently at the third tank. Evidently he saw nothing that told him anything, so he moved to the one next to me.

I looked for some way to lock this thing. There were two symbols on the inside of the door. Maybe one to lock or unlock and one to open. I hesitated, my finger over the red symbol. Maybe I'd be better off doing nothing than risking it.

I leaned toward the door, my hand ready to grab the handle to reclose the door and picked the other symbol. Something in my subconscious told me it was the right one, probably for no better reason than that it looked a little like the first letter in the Womper word for "protect."

I pushed it. The door stayed closed, and the color of the symbol changed to blue. I started breathing again.

Sam moved to the one I was in, his body now hidden by the opaque door.

I considered opening the door right then, very fast, but I might have knocked him off the catwalk and killed him. Now that I had protection like this I could afford to settle for disarming him.

I felt quite warm, but it probably was cooler in here than it was out where Sam was. The heat hadn't had time to penetrate the vehicles.

I looked at the controls. Sitting here wouldn't do me any good unless I could threaten Sam. And I had to hurry. Sam had seen the opening mechanism in the stalks. It wouldn't be long before he saw the parallel lines on these tanks.

The controls looked as if they could just as easily be for a starship or a cookie factory console as for a tank. I stared at them for a long moment before it came to me that actually most of them were indicators. The controls themselves were only a small fraction of what I was looking at.

I decided I didn't care about status—just results. The controls I could identify consisted of a joystick and a T-bar protruding from the console. The joystick handgrip was several sizes too large for me.

Experimentally, I moved the joystick. Nothing happened. I pulled on the T-bar. It seemed to be free to move easily in any direction but when I took my hands off it, it stayed exactly where it was. I could tilt it up and down, push it from side to side, twist the handle in circles, or push it farther into the console and then pull it back out. None of those variations did me any more immediate good than calisthenics. Nothing moved.

IV.

I'll Follow You Anywhere

I scanned the console, looking for a power switch. I finally found a candidate over my head on a panel of touch switches. The center switch was slightly larger than its neighbors, so I tried it.

For an instant, it seemed that the top half of the tank had

silently and instantaneously ejected. Sam loomed over me, looking almost straight at my face, but his expression was puzzled, unseeing. I reached toward him and my fingers brushed the door just where it had been before, but now everything above my stomach had turned transparent.

I looked up. Over my head the row of switches was apparently suspended in mid-air. I listened closely, to see if some new low whine had joined my breathing sounds, but it was utterly silent inside.

Sam was running his hand across the outside surface of the tank, so it must have still looked the same to him.

I tapped the control lever in his direction. The tank moved sideways as soon as I touched the control and stopped just as abruptly. It had moved about the width of a hand.

Sam jumped. He almost fell backward over the edge of the ramp, but he caught himself. It took him only a second to regain his composure to the point that he leveled his gun in my general direction.

I felt fairly secure in the tank, but safety seemed to be called for. I pushed the lever forward a little. The tank thudded against the one in front of it and slowed down. I pushed the lever farther.

It was almost like there was nothing in front of me. The tank moved forward smoothly and silently as the tank next in line was shoved into the one ahead of it, and then something gave, and the tank ahead slid off the side of the ramp, falling toward the floor.

I turned the control lever, and the tank rotated until I faced Sam. Sam was looking decidedly nervous.

I moved the tank forward, cutting the distance between us by a third. He turned and ran.

This was great. I hadn't had such a good time since I discovered sex.

Sam turned and ran between the next set of tanks, and I lost sight of him. It was only as I looked around, trying to decide which way to go next, that I realized I was at a slightly higher elevation than the tank next to me up the ramp.

Surprised, I tapped the lever upward. The tank rose straight into the air and hung there motionless, just under the next spiral of the ramp. I rotated the tank and launched it out into the air.

Suspended several levels from the ground, I turned the craft and saw Sam madly dashing along a catwalk. I pushed on the control stick and followed, rising as I went.

Sam reached a door and whipped it open. He didn't even close it behind him.

I hovered in front of the door, momentarily put off by the observation that the tank was slightly wider than the door. Then I thought about the joystick.

I gripped the control and found a trigger under my little finger. I squeezed it.

The room before me darkened abruptly, all except for the area around the door, which seemed to be a circle of normal illumination. Then the incandescence from the blast faded, and the light-control in the screen restored its normal transparency.

Where there had been a rectangular door, there was now a larger circular cutout exposing both the floor Sam had exited on and the floor below.

I moved through the opening and turned to follow Sam. He wasn't in sight. I pointed toward the intersection ahead and pushed hard on the control lever.

I overshot the intersection by probably half a block, nearly hitting the sides of the hall as I shot through it. I turned around and tried again more gently.

Sam was halfway down the next block, running toward the door we had used to enter the complex. I started to push on the stick to follow directly, and then I had a better, nastier idea. I suppose by this time I really was fairly irritated at him.

I swung back ninety degrees and shot down the hallway. This time I did a better job in estimating the force to use. I turned at the next intersection and headed parallel with Sam. At the next corner, I turned toward him again and deliberately slowed down before I got to the corner he had been running for.

I rotated the tank so I would be facing Sam and then nudged the tank abruptly into the intersection.

The expression on his face was worth the effort. He was no more than ten meters away, running as hard as he could toward me when I swung into his path. He slid to a halt, his face turning even redder than it already was, his eyes seeming twice as large as normal. I hadn't seen such raw panic since my last board meeting.

I tapped the control lever forward and cut the distance between us by half.

Sam started to turn to run away, but halted in mid-motion and clutched his chest. Deep wrinkles formed on his forehead as he grimaced. I couldn't tell if he made any sound or not, but he fell against the wall, bending double and sliding toward the floor.

The gun fell out of his hand and came to rest nearby. Sam collapsed on the floor and all movement stopped.

After a moment's hesitation, I let the tank settle to the ground. I started to open the door but took my hand away before completing the motion.

If I were Sam, confronted by something like this tank, I might put on a show just like this.

13

Moment of Truth

I.
Over My Dead Body

I sat there in the tank a moment longer, looking at Sam. A
pallor like that would be hard to fake, but Sam was a tricky
guy. If I went out to check, and he killed me, then the others
would have virtually no chance to get out if Sam had a
weapon like this tank to hunt them down with. I didn't doubt
at all that the tank had capabilities far beyond the basics I had
been able to figure out. No doubt it could sense heat, detect
motion—it was quiet enough that even audio sensing would
be effective.

I wondered about that. If I could figure out how to turn it
on, I could listen for Sam's heartbeat. Of course, with my
familiarity with the controls, I could just as easily eject
myself from the tank, maybe even squash myself into the
ceiling in the process.

Enough of this. I finally realized that the real reason I was
delaying was that I was afraid I had killed Sam. Another
death on my hands. Not that Sam was such a nice guy, but I
had intended only to shock him and then take him in to the
authorities. Being a funeral director's primary source of in-
come didn't appeal to me at all.

I pushed the unlock symbol on the door, and the panel

turned red. I pushed the symbol next to it, and the door opened.

"It's no good, Sam," I called. "Just get away from the gun, or I'll ram you."

Sam didn't respond.

I considered getting out of the tank and rejected the idea instantly. Instead, I closed and locked the door.

The gun lay near the center of the hall, perhaps an arm's length from Sam's outstretched hand. I pushed the lever forward lightly and moved well past Sam. When I looked back, the gun was still where it had been.

I turned around and tapped the lever down until I felt the thud of the tank hitting the floor. Idly I wondered if another strong tap would punch my way into the floor below. I moved toward Sam and the gun again, also applying a little downward pressure to make sure I didn't rise over the gun.

When I looked behind me the next time, the gun was no longer near Sam's hand. The corridor looked a bit different, too. There was a patch, about as wide as the tank, where the top layer of the floor had been stripped away, changing the texture from mottled black to a smooth, skinned look.

I lifted the tank up to about knee level, and hovered back toward Sam until I could see the floor below where I had stopped. The gun was there, next to a tidy section of floor material that had neatly rolled itself up.

I let the tank settle to the floor, door toward the gun. Sam still hadn't moved.

I opened the door, looking back to make sure Sam was still there, and got out quickly and retrieved the gun.

I looked around the edge of the tank, which from the outside still looked black, and saw Sam. He was sprawled next to the wall, looking dead.

"OK, Sam," I said, moving closer. "I've got this thing pointed at you. If you move, I'll use it."

I pointed it at the wall and made sure he hadn't somehow used it up or turned on a safety. The beam lanced into the wall and made a pinpoint glow.

When I got to Sam, I gave him a good kick in the leg. There was no response to a kick that should have given a living person quite a lot of pain.

One arm pointed out from his body, so I moved around

him until I was near it. Holding the gun pointed toward his chest, I felt for a pulse.

"Damn it all!" I yelled. "*Nobody* has heart attacks at your age, Sam. Except you."

The gun fell from my fingers as I slid down against the wall. I'd already spent enough time with my precautions that brain death was unavoidable. Another death. Damn, damn, damn. What would my father think of me now? I thought crazily.

I sat there a long time, next to Sam's cooling body, trying to make sense of it all. It never did seem to make a lot of sense. As I recovered a little, I remembered the floaters I had taken from the Womper. I might have been able to use them against Sam, but I had forgotten them entirely in my rush for the tank. And they might well have had the same result.

Finally I gave Sam as much of a temporary burial as I could. I dragged his body into one of the cubicle rooms. On the door, I used the gun to write "SAM."

Now to find the others. I got back in the tank and reoriented myself, turning the tank toward the center sphere.

I saw no one as I sped silently through the corridors.

I stopped before I got to the center, though. Another thought had been bothering me, but it was only now that I realized what it was. I found another cubicle room and made a close examination before I resumed my journey toward the sphere. I felt sick.

The door into the sphere was wide enough for me to get through in the tank without resorting to blasting my way in. It was just as well, because with my current load of anger and frustration, I would have. And there had already been enough senseless destruction.

There was no one visible in the sphere, so I flew toward the center. Between the two center stalks, I let the tank fall slowly to the floor. I took a deep breath before opening the door.

I didn't actually open it all the way, remembering Zeldon's quickness with a gun and forgetting that he no longer had a gun. I opened it far enough to yell through.

"It's me—Ben! I'm getting out, so don't anyone do anything dangerous!"

I opened the door the rest of the way and stepped out. It

was only then that I was aware of the pain in my shoulder again, but it was manageable.

"I said it's me!" I yelled louder. "Sam's not in there with a gun on me! He's dead!" I closed the door on the tank and displayed my gun.

From somewhere above came the sounds of rapid footsteps. "Ben!" It was Kate's voice.

From different directions came the sounds of others in the party. Soon I could see them coming from four distinct locations. Kate and Dr. Fenton and Rummel. And Zeldon.

Kate still had the energy to run to meet me. "Are you all right?" she asked.

"Mostly, I suppose."

"What does that mean?"

"I'll tell you in a few minutes." I stopped talking as the other three came closer.

"How did you get away from our follower, Zeldon?" I called.

"I didn't."

Sure enough, there it came behind him, maneuvering down the stairs.

"It was evidently never intended to harm us," Zeldon said. "It seems to be assigned to follow visitors around, maybe for monitoring their actions. It must have had fairly strong orders, though, to make it cut through walls."

"Am I glad to see you," Dr. Fenton said. "Now we can finally get out of this place."

"Not for a little while yet," I said.

"What do you mean?"

"It means," I said, pointing my gun at Zeldon, "that sometimes I think my IQ should be measured in parts per million. It means that Zeldon here has some things he wants to tell us. Don't you, Zeldon?"

II.

Confession Is Good for the Soul

"Ben?" Kate said, as though she was sure I was going crazy.

"*Now* what's going on?" Rummel said.

"Zeldon?" I prompted.

"What is it that you wish me to tell you? We are all fairly tired."

"You especially, Zeldon. You've been a busy person lately, haven't you?"

"I don't know what you're talking—"

"I'm talking about the life support!" Only after I cut him off did I realize how loudly I had shouted. I tried again, keeping my voice under rigid control. "I am talking about the suspended-animation, life-support mechanism that was keeping all these Wompers alive."

"Was?" Kate said.

"Tell me about it right now, Zeldon, or so help me, I'll have another act of senseless violence on my hands. Of course, it won't matter too much to you since you'll be dead."

"Ben, you're not thinking too clearly," Dr. Fenton said.

"Oh, but you're wrong there. I'm thinking clearly for the first time in several hours. How is it that Zeldon knows his way around in here so damn well? Why is it that, out of character by a kilometer, Zeldon didn't volunteer to deal with that follower the first time we had a run-in? And then why the rapid turnabout the second time? Who led us right to the control room? Why am I asking all these questions?"

The sphere was silent for a long moment.

"You're taking too long to answer, Zeldon. This is going to hurt you more than it hurts me."

Dr. Fenton said, "Ben, maybe you're jumping—"

Zeldon interrupted this time. "Ben, if I tell you what you want to know, will you promise to kill me?"

"What?"

"I know what I said. And I know what I've done." Zeldon sat down on the floor heavily and looked up at me. "I have just committed about ten million members of my own race to death.''

"There's still time, Zeldon. Reverse it." Zeldon and I were the only ones talking now. Everyone else must have been too stunned.

"I cannot. The damage cannot be repaired in time to save them.''

Now *I* was too stunned to say anything.

Finally I said, "Please tell me the truth, Zeldon. Is there really not time to save them?''

"I will tell you no more lies. Their time has run out. Finally.''

"I take it you knew about this place before we got inside?''

"No. That is, I knew that such places existed. I didn't know that one was here.''

"Such places," I said. "You mean like this ship?''

"Ship?" Kate said. "You're saying this is a ship?''

"He is correct," Zeldon said. "This is indeed a ship. One of three built long, long ago.''

"Tell us about it, Zeldon. Tell us how the Wompers have convinced the other races they paid no attention to the past when all along it sounds as though they paid far more attention than even humans did.''

"It is something I and my people are profoundly ashamed of.''

"I take it you mean the history, not the fact that you just killed ten million people?''

"Yes." Zeldon blinked his large eyes. "A long time ago, many thousands of years past, my people became infected. They were infected with a sickness deep in their souls. A group of my people became infatuated with power. No, maybe not 'infatuated.' Maybe 'love.' Or whatever word you choose to mean a total obsession with, seeing only the good side of, never the bad side.

"At first we paid them little attention. This group seemed to be encouraging an optimism, a pride in ourselves, a kind of feeling of self-worth that we had not had before. To some it seemed good. To others it seemed tolerable. And the infection spread.

"It spread for many centuries until the group became so

powerful that it controlled the rest of us rather than the reverse. And it became hateful.

"Wompers grew in power in our region of the universe. At first they extorted favors from other races, but as time went on they began to take what they wanted by force, caring less and less about the cost to other peoples. As with a wild animal crazed by the taste of blood, they escalated their efforts until they had neither friends nor allies.

"They, of course, wanted neither. They wanted power. Their weapons of war grew more forceful and mighty until they outstripped all the adversaries' forces. And finally they went too far. Too far for their enemies. And too far for us observers. They utterly destroyed two inhabited planets in the time it would take for a rest break during a negotiation session.

"Civil war began. It was the meek observers against the infected ones. The meek were unable to do enough themselves, but at the same time, every known race banded together for retribution. Together, we were enough to defeat the infected ones, but they were prepared for such a contingency. They activated emergency plans and fled in three enormous ships, each equipped with life-support systems good enough to let them sleep twenty to thirty thousand years. Until their enemies were dead.

"And the ships were equipped with vast weapon factories. The instruments of death you have seen under construction here are merely the equivalent of pocket knives in a hunter's collection."

"I don't understand something," Kate said. "What are the settlements we found outside?"

"I don't know for certain," Zeldon said, "but the most likely possibility is that some of the people who arrived here were not sympathizers, but rather people who came along rather than be put to death for resisting. I assume that once this facility had settled into place, they completed their escape plans and left secretly so they could live out their lives outside."

I said, "But what about the Wompers who were killed near the door that we blew open? Why were they there?"

"They probably came with measurement equipment to see why readings on the door indicated something abnormal.

With their defensive screens in place, they couldn't see out via instruments, but they could take local measurements. After such a terribly long time, those awake were probably arrogant enough to be incautious. We were just lucky that we killed several people on our way in. With only a few people awake at any one time, they were likely to be so bored that it didn't take much of a diversion to justify their investigating anything unusual, however small.''

"Oh," Kate said. "And I understand something else now. Ben, you talked about Zeldon being unwilling to take risks at first, but being willing later. You meant Zeldon damaged the suspended-animation controls while we were in this room the first time. Until he'd done that, he couldn't afford to die. Once he'd finished, it no longer mattered."

"Exactly. The way I figure it, Zeldon destroyed some backup equipment with his gun when we came in here, and then shut off the rest of the systems from the pod.''

Zeldon nodded.

"What about the other two ships?" she asked. "Have they been found?"

"No. But with this ship available for research, people can build defenses, perhaps even find a way to locate the other two. They won't be the vicious surprises that they would have been.''

"So you've recovered your honor, Zeldon?" I asked. "By killing ten million people?"

"One cannot recover what one never had to begin with. But I can die now knowing that I made a change in the world, a change that may let my children's children die at peace when their time comes.''

"Why the talk of *your* death?"

"Because it is time for me to die." Zeldon's eyes actually looked sad. "If, after I'm gone, you doubt the wisdom of what I have done, look through the archive in here. I am confident you will see many recorded scenes that will convince you of the unalterable evil in the people who resided here.''

Zeldon rose and started walking slowly toward me. "Please give me your weapon."

"Why?"

"I cannot live any longer with having killed. The pain is too great. I must depart."

"No, Zeldon. Hold it right there. That's no solution."

Zeldon kept moving closer. "You really have no choice, Ben. The only way you can stop me is to shoot me. And you will not do that."

I kept my gun pointing at him until he stood directly in front of me.

"I must have it," he said softly, and he twisted the gun out of my hand.

III.

Past the Point of No Return

Zeldon backed up with my gun in his hand. He surveyed the four of us. "Ben," he said, his tone of voice implying he had an afterthought. "The symbol of a 'V' and an upside-down 'V' superimposed is the learning indicator. You should be able to find out whatever you need that way." He gestured at the pods atop their stalks.

I opened my mouth to say something, but Zeldon cut me off. "I have done what I had to do, but I cannot live with such a burden of guilt. Ben, I knew of you before we met here. You are a good man, one who hates senseless killing. I trust you to know how to deal with what you learn in here. You will not let me down, will you?"

I shook my head no.

"Thank you, Ben. Thank you all," he said. Zeldon took a deep breath as he slowly adjusted the nozzle of the gun. When he was finished, he turned the muzzle toward his head and pulled the trigger.

Kate gasped as a thin, bright beam lanced out of Zeldon's head opposite the gun muzzle. I didn't feel too good myself.

Zeldon's body slumped heavily to the floor. One more death in the chain reaction.

I broke out of my trance and moved slowly to his body. I pulled my gun away from his fingers and wondered for a long moment if maybe that was the only way out. I hadn't deliberately killed as many people as Zeldon had, but what was the real difference between one and ten million? Did it matter whether it was deliberate or accidental?

"Don't do anything rash or stupid, Ben."

I looked up to see Kate standing next to me. I rose to stand beside her, wondering how she could know me so well in such a short time.

"OK. Nothing rash or stupid right now." I looked briefly at Dr. Fenton and Rummel. "Well, maybe nothing stupid at least."

"What do you mean?" Kate asked.

"I'll tell you in a minute. In the meantime, does anyone *else* have anything to confess?"

No one spoke.

"OK," I said, marshalling my strength. "What I meant was, what's one of the possible outcomes if we go out and report that there's a monumental supply of heavy weapons and undoubtedly valuable technology in here?"

"Suppression?" Kate said before Fenton or Rummel could open their mouths.

"Exactly. So I'm thinking we should do something that would make it utterly impossible to keep this ship a secret. And to guarantee that everyone gets an equal chance to have access to it."

Dr. Fenton looked perplexed. I guess he was at his best figuring out *old* puzzles.

Rummel and Kate were both favoring me with knowing looks, though. Kate said, "You mean take this ship on a short flight?"

"Right again."

It took Dr. Fenton only a few seconds to concur once he realized what we were going to do.

We went up to the control pods once again, one of us in each. I found the symbol Zeldon had told me about and it unlocked a wealth of information. There was even water available in the pods. Before long we understood at least the basics of the communications and shielding subsystems. Eventually we understood simple functions of the drive. The weapons system was more complex, but at least we knew how to avoid it.

After a long exploration of the commands and controls, I was feeling so good that I realized I was hungry. It's funny how your priorities shift.

"Are we ready?" I said at last.

Three voices told me we were.

"OK. Here goes the barrier." I pushed on the correct symbol, and several lights changed color instantly. The screen showed a view of outside now that the absence of the barrier permitted *us* to see out.

"Let's see what's outside the main door," Kate said, taking actions in her pod. Now on the screen was a view of workers busily positioning another device outside the door.

"I think a little communication is in order," I said, pressing the correct indicators.

"Can you hear me out there?" I asked a moment later.

Heads popped up in the tunnel outside. I saw several mouths open and a few heads nod.

"Good. We are all right. This is Ben Takent. Kate Dunlet, Dr. Fenton, and Rummel Hurdt are all here and in good shape. The others are with us. We know now how to open the door, but it's going to be dangerous for anyone who's in the tunnel or next to Vandict Butte. Please clear the area immediately. Don't let anyone remain nearer than a half-kilometer to the butte." What was one little white lie after having killed so many people?

They started clearing the area. It took almost half an hour before they were out, but when we swept the entire perimeter, we saw no one in what we considered to be the danger region.

"Are we ready for takeoff?" I asked. "Are your seat belts fastened and your tray tables in their upright positions?"

"We're ready, *co*-pilot," Kate said.

"Let's do it then." I had already entered the initial leg of our flight plan—rise vertically to the Womper equivalent of one thousand meters. I punched the symbol on the panel.

There was no sound. And no motion at first. The view on the screen was split into five sections, showing various views of the outside. They were all stable.

Then a rumbling noise began, and we started to move. The view of the tunnel showed the reinforced roof coming loose and falling.

In the other cameras, dust began to conceal some of the images. I punched up other views. Through one we saw what looked to be the view from underneath a waterfall except that the falling matter consisted of rocks, boulders, and dust.

"Damn it!" I said a moment later. "Now I'll have to pay for a new camera."

After the intense acceleration in the tubes and elevators, I was surprised at the mildness of the lift-off.

Another view came on the screen, looking straight down below us into the hole we had left behind. I wished I could have seen the expressions on those watching from the distance as the entire Vandict Butte lifted into the air and the thin butte sides slid away to fall into a square of rubble. It was like flying a small planet.

"We have ignition!" came Dr. Fenton's gleeful cry, surprising me almost as much as anything else had in the last several hours.

In actual fact, we didn't have ignition, but it would have been churlish to point that out. The ship's drive must have been a big brother of the tank's drive. We just hung there at one thousand meters, the view below us unobstructed as the dust slowly swirled and settled.

I switched on the transmitter which we had earlier set up for compatibility with the spaceport outside Dallad. "You want to do the honors, Kate?"

"Sure." She took control and began speaking. "Attention, Dallad Control. Request to land two kilometers to the west of the port. Do you read me?" She wasn't successful in keeping the laughter out of her voice.

After a delay, a voice sounded inside the pod. "This is Dallad Control. I read you. Identify yourself."

"This is the starship *Vandict*. Repeat, request to land two kilometers west of the port."

"You want to land a *starship*? What kind of joke is this?"

"It's no joke," Kate said. "Our estimated time of arrival is ten minutes from now. I assume you'll be ready."

"We warned them," I said, pushing the next symbol to begin the flight.

The viewer below us showed our enormous shadow begin to move fluidly over the remains of the butte and then over the dig. Our shadow dwarfed the site and provided the first shade they'd had there for quite a while.

I watched the screen showing us the forward view. I wasn't too worried about filing a flight plan. People could probably see us halfway to Dallad. And if someone were crazy enough to deliberately fly into us, we weren't likely even to feel a bump.

"I say again," came the voice from Dallad Control. "Who are you? Practical jokes will be dealt with—Holy Mother!" He must have just seen our radar profile enter his screen. There was a sound something like that of a chair being knocked backward, and then the microphone on the other end went silent.

Dr. Fenton laughed out loud.

I said, "The rules for landing starships are probably in his other suit."

A new voice came on the speaker. She said, "This is Dallad Control. You have permission to land two kilometers west of the port. Please identify yourselves and your planet of origin."

"We're local," I said. "That is, we weren't born here, but we've all been living here."

"All? How many are there of you?"

"Somewhere between four and maybe ten million," I said.

IV.
I Always Wanted to Do That

We gently landed approximately where we had said we would. With a craft that size, it's hard to be precise.

When we had shut down the flight system, Dr. Fenton read a prepared speech explaining who we were and why we were there. When he was finished, he told them that the door would open only when there were on hand senior representatives from each race, all empowered to speak for their elements of the government.

We couldn't have got a committee to agree any faster even if they were voting on their next pay raise.

14

How Did I Know
It Would End Up Like This?

I.

I'm Glad You Asked That

The sun above Dallad beat down on me as though it were trying to catch up for the time I had spent inside the ship cut off from its influence. I felt caught up already. The heat-exchanger people were promising to be available Real Soon Now. Maybe I could snoop around and find something I could use to blackmail them into coming out immediately. That is, if I wanted to snoop. At the moment, I was unsure whether I was in the right profession.

I walked through the crowd in East Market, oblivious to all but the loudest kids and the people who bumped into me as I pushed forward.

Some time later, I found a shaded chair with a view to the west. I could see in the distance the convoy of vehicles carrying Womper bodies to what would probably be the largest mass burial since that group had fled and hidden.

Zeldon had done his work on the suspended-animation system correctly. No one had survived. The best the authorities' experts had been able to do was eventually turn the cooling back on so the bodies could be moved out slowly.

Zeldon had told us the truth. The recordings inside the ship revealed a legacy of death and destruction, showing all too vividly what that branch of his race had been like. The recordings were a little like the video memoirs that might have been left behind by a serial-murderer, except these were on a massive scale. Cities instead of individuals, civilizations instead of families.

One of the recordings which had made it onto the local news showed a before-and-after on a densely populated world. The "after" displayed what looked to be a small volcanic flow with steaming molten rock churning and bubbling. The field of view pulled back and back and back until it encompassed the entire, glowing planet.

I was still sitting there minutes or hours later when a voice broke me out of the spell.

"What are you doing here, bug eye?"

I looked away from the distant view and saw Berto, his dark eyes wide and curious. "Just watching the procession," I said.

"What, those trucks? That's boring, man. Oh, I get it. You're on another case."

"No way."

"You're kidding. After all the times you've been on the news lately, you should have lots of business."

"I've had some offers. I just don't know if I want to take them."

Berto took a seat near me, staying just out of the shade. "I don't get it. What's the problem?"

"I don't think you'd under—" I hesitated. "Who knows? Maybe you *would* understand. Have you ever done anything you felt guilty about? I don't need to know what it was."

"Maybe once." Berto grinned.

"Those people. The ones in those trucks down there. They might still be alive if it weren't for me."

"You're feeling guilty about that? The news said they deserved to die after all they did. And you didn't do it anyway. That Zeldon guy did. You know, the Womper who went in with you guys."

"OK. I guess I'm getting to the point where I can accept that. But I killed a couple of people on this case. Me, personally."

"You want to talk about it?"

As I considered his question, I looked back through the dusty sunshine at the distant caravan, and I felt tired. Tankur's endless day has a way of tricking you into thinking you cease to age once you reach here, but I suddenly felt older than I had when I arrived.

Finally I said, "I guess the only death I can feel better about is Elliot Pardo's. He was a guard at the dig. It turns out I didn't actually kill him."

"If you didn't kill him, why do you feel bad about him dying?"

"Because Sam used me to arrange his death." I explained who Sam was. "When the police searched Sam's place they found a supply of unusual needles. They dissolve after shooting an unhealthy amount of a hard-to-detect drug in the victim. So when I started talking to Elliot, Sam shot him with something that first overstimulated his aggression center and then killed him. Elliot was already angry when I met him; Sam must have told him some tale about me. It must have been Sam, too, who planted the artifact for me to find in Elliot's apartment."

"You're going too fast. What artifact?" Berto shifted position on his chair.

"An artifact that Sam and Elliot probably had in a stash someplace. They had to have been stealing artifacts from the dig before they were catalogued and placed in a vault. They never had anything to do with Harry Gatlon. Yeah, I know. You don't know who Harry Gatlon is. He's a guy who found another site that contained artifacts. He was digging them up to sell later, but another guy named Artemus found his stash and sold a couple of items from it. I thought—"

"You're making this way too complicated, man."

"OK. Let me do it another way. Sam and Elliot were stealing. When Sam heard about an artifact showing up in town, one that it turns out Artemus sold, Sam probably figured Elliot was cheating him. The only solution was to kill him so Elliot couldn't make a blunder and expose Sam. Sam could have killed him outright, but he would have had to risk calling attention to himself. So he maneuvered me into thinking I was the one who killed him.

"So the death I took the hardest at first wasn't even my fault. But Sam's death, the death I caused the most recently, could have been avoided if I hadn't been so angry at him. Maybe it's some kind of cosmic justice. If Sam hadn't killed Elliot, I wouldn't have been maneuvered into killing Sam. And Zeldon killed himself because he couldn't face the responsibility. Other than the Wompers inside, that just leaves Harry Gatlon. And Harry wouldn't have died if he hadn't tried to kill me.''

"How did you kill this Harry Gatlon?"

I told Berto about the events that occurred after Artemus had showed me the artifacts. I could still see Gatlon's blood oozing into the dry arroyo dust.

II.

How I Spent My Summer Excavation

When I finished talking, Berto said, "You know what I think, bug eye? I think you're still making all this too complicated."

"I know it's confusing. But everything is related to everything else."

"No. I don't mean that. I mean you did what you had to do. If you thought it was wrong, you wouldn't have done it, or if you *meant* to do something wrong, you wouldn't be worrying about it now. So you must be an OK guy, man. Simple."

I was about to tell Berto he was simplifying too much, but suddenly I wasn't sure he was. In that moment I realized, despite the remorse I felt over the deaths, that I still did believe I had done the right thing.

I had been vaguely aware of the people passing nearby, but as I looked back at the caravan, my field of view unconsciously widened, and my eyes now saw more than only a tunnel-vision view ahead. I was suddenly aware of all the activity on the periphery. It was as if I had just awakened from a disturbing dream.

"Berto, maybe you're older than I thought you were," I said at last. "Or maybe you're right. Maybe I do try to make things more complicated than they need to be."

"Don't worry about it. I think all adults do the same thing."

I actually felt better. "Thanks. I wish there was some way I could pay you back."

"You already did. The reward money, remember? I told you you were an OK guy." Berto grinned, and I grinned right back at him.

"You going to be all right, bug eye?" he asked.

"Yeah. I think so."

"I'll see you around then, right?"

"Count on it."

Down the street were a few of Berto's friends. He rose and started running to meet them. Halfway there, he turned and waved. I waved back.

After a few minutes, I touched my new wristcomp and turned calls back on.

As I sat there, still shielded from the sun, I made yet another realization thanks to this frenzy of introspection. I missed the stars. Fixed on the sunny-side-up face of Tankur, I saw only the one bright, fiery star. I missed the cool expanse and the blackness between the distant stars. I longed for the night.

And I missed another thing. I missed the changes—day after night—season after season. With no transitions, no obvious cosmic clock to divide the fragments of my life, it seemed that time was passing me by like some speck on a never-changing sundial. Talk about your petty pace from day to day.

I was still sitting in the shade, lost in thought, when my wristcomp sounded.

"This is Ben Takent," I said.

"Mr. Takent, I've been trying to reach you," came a familiar voice from the speaker. "My name is Morgan, and I wanted to schedule a time to talk to you about your life insurance needs—"

Morgan. The idiot who had left so many messages that he forgot who had been calling whom. "Morgan, cross me off your list, OK? You call me one more time and we'll be talking about *your* life insurance needs." I switched off.

A moment later I realized that, despite the short flash of irritation, I was still smiling.

And why shouldn't I be? I could still talk tough, and I had done the best I could. Ten thousand years ago, the desert out there had been simple dust and rocks. Now it was once again. From dust to dust.

If only this dustball of a planet could travel from dusk to dusk.

Suddenly unsure whether I had been hanging around East Market for minutes or days, I rose and stepped out into the bright, unvarying sunlight. I turned toward home, suspecting that I would find Kate waiting there. I took a deep breath and picked up my pace.

Even if she wasn't at home or the office, I was confident I could find her. After all, despite late-night slurs from a man now dead, I *am* a private detective.